CHASING THE VIOLET KILLER

R. BARRI FLOWERS

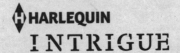

HARLEQUIN
INTRIGUE

In memory of my beloved mom, Marjah Aljean, who inspired me
to be my best and was a longtime fan of Harlequin romances. To
Loraine, the love of my life, who has never allowed me to stop
believing in myself, and to the many fans of my romance, mystery
and thriller fiction over the years. Lastly, a nod goes out to editors
Allison Lyons and Denise Zaza for the opportunity to lend my
voice and creative spirit to the Intrigue line.

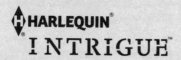

HARLEQUIN®
INTRIGUE™

PLEASE RECYCLE · THIS PRODUCT IS RECYCLABLE

Recycling programs
for this product may
not exist in your area.

ISBN-13: 978-1-335-48936-4

Chasing the Violet Killer

Copyright © 2021 by R. Barri Flowers

This edition published by arrangement with Harlequin Books S.A.

For questions and comments about the quality of this book,
please contact us at CustomerService@Harlequin.com.

Harlequin Enterprises ULC
22 Adelaide St. West, 41st Floor
Toronto, Ontario M5H 4E3, Canada
www.Harlequin.com

Printed in U.S.A.

R. Barri Flowers is an award-winning author of crime, thriller, mystery and romance fiction featuring three-dimensional protagonists, riveting plots, unexpected twists and turns and heart-pounding climaxes. With an expertise in true crime, serial killers and characterizing dangerous offenders, he is perfectly suited for the Intrigue line. Chemistry and conflict between the hero and heroine, attention to detail and incorporating the very latest advances in criminal investigations are the cornerstones of his romantic suspense fiction. Discover more on popular social networks and Wikipedia.

Books by R. Barri Flowers

Harlequin Intrigue

Chasing the Violet Killer

Visit the Author Profile page at Harlequin.com.

CAST OF CHARACTERS

Naomi Lincoln—The Secret Service special agent returns home to Pebble Creek, Oregon, to bury the uncle she witnessed being murdered on her laptop. She finds herself drawn into the police investigation into a serial killer with the lead detective, her ex-boyfriend.

Dylan Hester—A homicide detective for the Pebble Creek PD, he is tasked with catching a serial killer while protecting the woman who left him heartbroken. Can he keep her safe and win back her love?

Patricia Stabler—The FBI special agent and criminal profiler is determined to solve this case for the Bureau. Persuading Naomi to take an active role in the investigation makes sense, but could it backfire?

Zachary Jamieson—The florist has a passion for violets, a criminal record and is a primary suspect as the killer. Has he taken things to the next level as a serial murderer?

Roger Lincoln—The retired police investigator turned private eye was killed in pursuit of a murderer. Can he still help solve the case from the grave?

The Violet Killer—The elusive serial killer of local women leaves a single violet as a calling card. Will Naomi become his next strangulation victim?

Prologue

They had become far too predictable. The nice-looking, shapely young women would leave themselves open to whatever—or whoever—came their way, as if they had not a care or concern in the world. Whether it was jogging for no good reason, walking by their lonesome in the dead, dark of night, being utterly lackadaisical in an unattended parking garage, stupidly leaving a car unlocked, a window open or other avoidable means of vulnerability, they were ripe for the picking, like a perfect and delicious red apple. Or even a green one—that worked for him, too. It made his mission almost too easy for someone who liked challenges. Not that he had anything against hardly having to work to satisfy his cravings, per se. Why should he care if the pretty, sexy ones fell right into his trap like enticing lambs to the slaughter? Wasn't that what every sensible and eager serial killer dreamed of?

He broke free of his admittedly dark reverie, recognizing that the moment at hand was quickly approaching. It wouldn't be very smart if his own overconfidence and, frankly, lack of scruples cost him another victim to add to his lovely collection of violets. There she was. Just like clockwork. Ticktock. Ticktock. He remained hidden and motionless in the shadows, watching excitedly as she tied her long and curly raven hair in a ponytail, adjusted her earbuds and set off running in colorful designer jogging attire. On the surface, the wooded area full of Douglas firs and Western white pines seemed safe enough, even during twilight hours, with lamps giving off just enough light and other runners to pass by for a sense of security. He assumed that was the runner's calculus, false as it was. Perhaps she planned to meet her husband or boyfriend afterward for dinner and sex or whatever. Or maybe she would settle for a nice hot shower and good night's sleep, before starting the boring work grind all over again tomorrow.

Unfortunately, she would never live to see another day. Or even an hour. She had seen to that herself. She was like a cornered and helpless rat, and it was time to take out of its misery by going in for the kill. Anticipating her every move like a champion chess player who had an aversion to losing, he was faster and smarter, enabling him to beat her to the point where she would normally have veered off to the left and another, more active jogging trail.

Instead, he was waiting for her there, flexing an expensive silk scarf as a prelude to what was coming. The terrified look on her pretty face and in those big, brown eyes was almost worth the satisfaction welling within him like a furnace ready to erupt. Almost.

It wasn't till she tried halfheartedly in a moment of desperation to escape the trap that he had set that he cut her off and made sure her attempt fell like a flattened tire. Before any screams could erupt from her full mouth, he had already wrapped the scarf around her neck, twisting and tightening with pleasure in silencing her till her last breath was expended. Only then could he breathe a sigh of relief that he had succeeded in killing once again.

As the victim sank down to the ground, he pulled out a single blue violet and stuck it between her lips that had remained parted even in death, as if welcoming his going-away-from-life present.

Chapter One

"We just got a report of a man being shot at an office building on Seventeenth and Bedford," the 911 dispatcher said tensely. "The victim has been identified as Roger Lincoln..."

Detective Dylan Hester's heart sank into his stomach as the name smacked him like a solid punch in the gut. Roger Lincoln was a former homicide detective for the Pebble Creek Police Department in the quaint Oregon town eighty-five miles south of Portland. Dylan canceled plans to stop by Lesley's Restaurant on Crome Street for a slice of homemade apple pie in lieu of lunch, and immediately headed straight to the scene—unsure if it was a crime, accident, suicide or attempted suicide. He hated to think any was the case, all things considered. A criminal act of violence would certainly be a hard pill to swallow. Especially at this stage of the game for the retiree. An accidental shooting of himself, as someone experienced with firearms, was hard to fathom. But wanting to check out on his own terms was no less painful to contemplate. Yet, for one reason or another, the man had shockingly been a victim of gunfire...

"I'm just two blocks away, Lily," Dylan told the dispatcher, ill at ease, hoping against hope that they weren't dealing with a fatality here.

Roger Lincoln had been his partner, mentor and good friend. He'd been someone Dylan had continued to rely on for advice even after Roger's sudden retirement last year at the relatively young age of fifty-eight. When his bad back made it impossible to do his job effectively, rather than take a desk job stacking papers, as someone who loved being out in the field as an investigator, Roger chose to walk away with his pension and pride intact after nearly thirty years on the force. He had remained connected to the department as a consultant on the Violet Killer case. A serial killer was strangling attractive young women, disturbingly leaving a single blue violet in their mouths as his calling card.

The case had been laid squarely on Dylan's lap as the youngest but most accomplished member of the homicide unit, at thirty-three years of age. A decorated veteran and former member of the US Army Special Operations force, he'd served in Afghanistan and Iraq, and had a bachelor's degree in criminal justice and master's in criminology. Not that professional and educational achievement or persistence had done him much good as yet in tracking down the cunning killer. Thus far, he had murdered seven local women over two short years—the latest victim just two days ago—in various locations and remained elusive as ever, in spite of the painstaking efforts of the Pebble Creek PD, working in conjunction with the Federal Bureau of Investigation, Oregon State Police and Blane County Sheriff's Department to identity the perpetrator and bring him to justice for his crimes. Could Roger, who had made no secret of his desire to get the Violet Killer as his going-away present to the department and doing right by the victims and the loved ones they left behind, have homed in on the killer's identity, thereby making him a threat that needed to be neutralized?

Dylan swallowed that chilling thought and asked Lily, "Who reported the incident?"

"The caller identified herself as the victim's niece, Naomi Lincoln. Apparently, she was having a video chat on the computer with him when the shooting occurred—"

That unexpected revelation threw Dylan for a loop, leaving him even more unsettled and causing the car to jerk toward oncoming traffic before he managed to regain control. Naomi Lincoln. He could only imagine the horror of what she must have witnessed before her very eyes. The name rang in his head as though surrounded by flashing lights, spurring a wave of emotions in Dylan, as someone he had tried hard to forget, failing miserably in that impossible endeavor. Naomi Rachel Lincoln happened to be his ex-girlfriend and almost fiancée, who had stunningly and inexplicably tossed aside what he'd thought was a love match made in Pebble Creek, if not heaven and earth, in favor of joining the US Secret Service two years ago. It broke his heart in more places than one, not to mention his spirit, when she told him the opportunity was simply too much to pass up. Even if it meant ending their relationship then and there. She did just that, without apparently much hesitation or looking back once she was fast out the door, leaving him high and dry.

Rather than try to talk her out of it—not sure he could have, even with what he considered pretty damned good powers of persuasion, given her own stubbornness and strong determination—Dylan did what he thought was the honorable thing, if not the most foolish, as a man who'd fallen in love with the biracial and shapely beauty who had him tied up in knots. He took a step back, maybe a few steps, wished her well and tried to get on with his life, hard as it would be without her in it. But pretending she didn't exist at all—a herculean task—was never in the cards. Through Roger, he'd kept tabs on Naomi and her burgeoning career in Miami. By all accounts, she was truly in her element as a Secret Service special agent, assigned to the investigation detail in building upon her previous career with the county as a crime victims service coordinator. But Roger had been quick to point out, whether Dylan wanted to hear it or not, that she wasn't seeing anyone seriously as far as he knew, as if to leave that window open for them to someday get back together.

Even if a small part of him found much appeal in that possibility, Dylan didn't see that happening, as too much time had passed and neither seemed

willing to give up the lives they had carefully con-
structed like a well-built fortress on opposite sides
of the country. He wouldn't ask or expect her to do
what he wasn't willing to do himself. Some things
simply weren't meant to be. He was sure this was
one of them.

He pulled his unmarked dark-colored vehicle into
the parking lot on Bedford Avenue of the three-story
brick building that housed Roger's office. A squad
car, its lights flashing, and a detective's cruiser were
already at the scene. Dylan could hear the siren of
an ambulance approaching. He raced inside and ran
up one flight of stairs and down a long hall, turning
to the right at the end, with a shorter hall that led
to the second-floor office he'd visited several times
since Roger set up his private detective and consultant agency, Lincoln Investigations.

An officer was standing guard at the door, looking grim. Dylan showed his identification. His deep
molten-gray eyes rose over the officer's wide shoulders and spotted the detective inside. Apparently,
they weren't dealing with an active gunman still on
the scene to prevent Roger from getting treatment.
But there may have been more than one victim.

"How many people are injured?" Dylan asked the
officer just to be sure.

"Just one," he said tonelessly.

"Still one too many," Dylan grumbled, as knots
churned in his stomach, which often happened when
he had a bad feeling about something.

He stepped inside the midsized office, cluttered

with folders on top of folders Dylan knew were files on national cold cases Roger consulted on or hoped to. There was a double-hung window overlooking the street. Careful not to contaminate what may be a crime scene as he walked across vinyl composite tile flooring, Dylan sidestepped potential evidence and was met halfway by his friend and colleague Detective Gregory Hwang.

"Hey," he said, his voice level. "Just beat you here."

"What have we got?" Dylan asked routinely, though knowing this was anything but routine. He glanced over at Roger Lincoln, who was sitting motionless in a high-backed ergonomic leather chair. His upper body was slumped over one side of an L-shaped wooden desk as if he had fallen asleep. Something told Dylan that he wasn't waking up anytime soon. If ever.

Hwang, a thinly built, seven-year veteran with short black hair and a heavy-stubble beard, was South Korea born, pushing forty and a single father of twin eight-year-old girls. He had been on the Violet Killer case from the start. Furrowing his forehead in three places presently, he confirmed Dylan's worst fears when he said, "There's no other way to say this, Dylan… Lincoln's gone…"

Dylan offered no response, though he was certain his dour expression said it all. How could this have happened? Did he really want to know? No, he needed to. He approached the desk and got a closer look. Roger's head lay in a pool of his own blood, soaking into thinning gray hair that was raggedly swept to one side. There was what looked to be a massive gunshot wound to his temple, marring the hardened, contorted features of his dark-skinned face. If he had to make a guess, based on his knowledge of firearms and their capabilities, Dylan would bet that the weapon used was a .45 ACP pistol. It appeared that a single shot was fired at point-blank range.

"Any sign of the firearm?" Dylan asked, while gazing at the blood-splattered floor around the desk.

"Not yet." Hwang flexed one of his hands covered by a nitrile glove. "I'm pretty sure we're not looking at a suicide here, if that's what you're thinking."

"I wasn't." Dylan knew for a fact that, since retiring, Roger favored a Ruger Blackhawk .44 Magnum revolver as his weapon of choice. This meant that the killer most likely used his or her own weapon to commit the crime. "Whoever did this was obviously smart enough not to leave the gun just lying around." Seeing no sign of Roger's weapon, Dylan figured the killer took it, too.

Even with the stark reality that this was murder, Dylan felt somewhat relieved that they weren't looking at a suicide, knowing Roger as he did. His differences with Naomi aside, Dylan wouldn't have wanted her to have to deal with such a crushing blow of Roger dying by his own hand. Not that the cold-blooded murder of Naomi's uncle would be any easier for her to deal with.

"Could we be looking at an attempted or completed robbery?" Hwang asked, not sounding as if he believed this.

"I doubt it. Robbers don't usually expect to find a pot of gold in a private detective's office." Dylan pinched his nose thoughtfully. "No, this was personal." Just how personal, he wasn't quite sure yet, but he had his suspicions.

Hwang cocked a brow. "You think it had something to do with a case he was working on?"

"That's what we need to find out," Dylan said, remaining noncommittal for the time being. "Better get the crime scene unit in here," he muttered bleakly.

"They're on their way, even as we speak," Hwang pointed out expectantly. "Whatever went down in this office and for whatever reason, Roger Lincoln didn't deserve to die this way. He was one of us and we'll do it by the book in solving this case as quickly as possible."

Dylan nodded, knowing the detective was just as up to the task as he was in dealing with a violent criminal act that needed to be properly investigated till its closure. Out of the corner of his eye, Dylan spotted something shiny beneath Roger's desk. Donning a pair of nitrile gloves, he bent down and grabbed it. It was a shell casing. Gazing at the manufacturer's marking, he saw that it corresponded with his estimate on the type of weapon used to shoot Roger. Holding up the spent casing, Dylan said, "Looks like the shooter left something behind after all."

"Sloppy," Hwang expressed, pleased, while presenting an evidence bag for Dylan to drop the casing into.

He did just that, while imagining the horrific moment of impact for Roger. "Either that, or the perp just didn't give a damn, figuring we wouldn't know what to do with it."

Hwang sneered. "Let him keep thinking that."

"We need to know who's come in and out of this building in the past hour," Dylan told the detective. "Hopefully, there are security cameras that can help us pinpoint Lincoln's killer, giving us the tools to fill in the blanks of identifying the perp."

Hwang concurred. "I spotted at least one surveillance camera when I came in. Apart from that, there seemed to be plenty of other people entering and exiting the building during the lunch hour, besides the killer. Chances are one or more saw something…or someone suspicious…"

"Maybe," Dylan said, having reservations about just how quickly they could solve this case. Most people simply weren't that observant when it came to paying attention to those around them. A clever perp could practically introduce him or herself to unsuspecting passersby and still not stand out. Dylan hoped that wasn't the case here, but he wasn't holding his breath on that front. He looked at an empty spot in the center of the desk where Roger's laptop had been, judging by the dust that formed a perfect rectangle. Had the killer stolen the computer? If so, why? Was something incriminating on it that might lead right to the perp's proverbial front door?

"Yeah, I noticed the laptop was missing, too," Hwang said, jutting his chin. "Looks like Roger's cell phone has also vanished. Pretty suspicious, huh?"

"It's much more than that," Dylan told him regrettably. "Roger was apparently video chatting on the laptop with Naomi when he was shot—"

"Seriously?" Hwang's jaw dropped with disbelief. "Sorry about that, man." He paused. "Have you talked to her about it?" Hwang was aware of his history with Roger's niece and that she was the adored child Roger never had, as well as someone who had worked with the police department in her former capacity.

"Not yet." Dylan drew a ragged breath. "I wanted to get more information before I called her." It wasn't a conversation he was particularly looking forward to, no matter the way things ended between them, but one that had to be done.

"Do what you need to do," Hwang said understandingly, "difficult as it will be. I can handle things here till the medical examiner and forensic team arrive."

"Thanks." Dylan shifted the weight of his tall, firm frame from one foot to the other, while pondering the possibility that Naomi may have critical information on the shooting, beyond the lethal act itself. Did Roger say anything to her that could have led to his death? Did she see or hear the shooter? Did the perp see her on the laptop screen? Whichever scenario Dylan played in his mind, it rattled him. The last thing he wanted was for Naomi to not only be a witness to murder but also be in potential danger herself. Though she was presumably still safely away in Miami, something told him that wouldn't be for long. Even if it was too late to save Roger, she would undoubtedly be returning to Pebble Creek to bury her uncle. Dylan was pretty sure there was nothing he could do or say to make Naomi stay put while the investigation into his death was underway, whether he wanted that or not.

He peered at Roger's disfigured face, or more specifically, at his lips that had turned wickedly purple. They were slightly open with blood spilling out of a corner. There seemed to be something inside the mouth. Still wearing the nitrile gloves, Dylan carefully parted Roger's lips and pulled out a saliva-moistened and bloodied violet.

"I'VE GOT A rock-solid lead on the so-called Violet Killer that has dogged me since retirement…" were the last words Secret Service Special Agent Naomi Lincoln's uncle, Roger Lincoln, uttered before she heard what sounded like a gunshot. Aghast, she watched him keel over as blood gushed from a gaping wound on the side of his head. A shadowy figure moved behind him, staying just out of view on the small screen of her laptop, before it went totally black.

In spite of being overwhelmed with emotion, while feeling utterly helpless to the moment at hand, Naomi had immediately called 911 to report the crime. Though she prayed that her uncle could somehow survive the atrocious and cowardly attack, she feared it was too late to save him. Before her very horror-struck, bold hazel eyes, someone—maybe this Violet Killer—had attacked the man who had raised her alone since she was ten years old after losing his brother, Milton, who was Naomi's father, and her mother, Paula, in a terrible head-on car collision. That was twenty years ago. Now, at thirty and an only child, Naomi was faced with the real possibility of having no more family she could lean on and give the same solid support in return.

It was this frightening prospect that weighed heavily on her mind as Naomi stood barefoot on the cold cherry micro-beveled hardwood flooring in the sunken living room of her downtown Miami, Florida, apartment. She shared the place with fellow Secret Service agent Sophia Menendez, currently on assignment out of state. Naomi turned her thoughts back to the serial killer who had terrorized Pebble Creek over the last two years. She hadn't kept up much with the case, other than knowing that a madman in the vein of the Boston or Hillside Stranglers was strangling to death local women and leaving a violet behind, while apparently taunting the authorities and daring them to stop him. When her uncle had retired, Dylan Hester had been assigned as lead investigator of the case. Last she knew, the killer was still very much at large. Had he changed his MO and gone after the man who was the closest thing she had to a father for two decades?

Naomi looked at the cell phone chiming in her

hand. The caller ID identified the person request-
ing a video chat as none other than Dylan himself.
A quiver shot through her as thoughts about him
flooded her head. He was once the love and lover of
her life and someone she'd envisioned a real future
with, where the commitment to each other stood the
test of time and with it came children to cement their
bond. But something happened that threw her fantasies entirely out of whack. Or at least those pertaining to Dylan. A remarkable opportunity arose two
years ago to join the United States Secret Service.
All things considered, professionally speaking, it was
an opportunity she could not turn her back on, hard
as it was on her personal and romantic life. It would
enable her to take a few giant steps toward using
her knowledge on crime victims to foster a career
in which she was able to go after those who would
seek to victimize others through money laundering,
counterfeiting and financial institution fraud, among
other serious crimes. Now she had to wonder if she
could do it over, would she? Naomi closed her eyes
for a moment while considering this, before opening
them. The answer was yes, even though with a heavy
heart. The truth was that while her uncle Roger took
Dylan under his wing, allowing his life in law enforcement to take off, her own career choices were
limited at best had she stayed in Pebble Creek. Her
uncle wisely recognized this and—though he understood it would likely mean an end to her involvement
with Dylan, given the long-distance relationship neither she nor Dylan wanted—encouraged Naomi to

pursue other paths to the success she deserved and her parents would have approved of, which she did. The painful trade-off was that it meant sacrificing her love life, not knowing if she would ever meet the likes of a Dylan Hester again. Or if she would even try.

Naomi hesitated to answer the phone, knowing what came next would rock her world, one way or another. She wiped tears from her golden-complexioned high cheeks, courtesy of the genetics of a white mother and African American father. Accepting the call, she saw Dylan's face appear. "Hey…" she uttered nervously.

"Hey." The timbre of his voice was still as richly deep and soothing as Naomi remembered. Her ex-boyfriend's ruggedly handsome, well-defined features had also changed little since she last saw him. His raven hair was in a newer square cut bordering an oblong face that was clean-shaven, but the gray eyes with flecks of brown and gold were just as intense as before.

Naomi trained her eyes on him, eager for information, knowing the nature of the first direct communication between them in over a year. Her heart raced. "Is my uncle Roger—" Her voice broke, unable to complete the question.

Dylan's forehead furrowed. "Roger didn't make it," he voiced sadly, while being direct. "I'm so sorry, Naomi."

Even suspecting as much before hearing the words, the pain of confirming her worst fears wasn't any less throbbing. Her knees wobbled, but she resisted sitting down. "Did you get the person responsible?" The query made it clear that she knew this was cold-blooded murder and not a self-inflicted gunshot fatality. Her uncle—who had never married, choosing his career over being in a committed relationship—loved life as much as he could. Even in retirement, with a bad back and a little crankiness, he would never have considered taking such a terrible course of action, to leave her to remember him in that awful way.

Dylan's eyes lowered lamentably. "As yet, we have no one in custody in connection with Roger's death."

Naomi wrinkled her dainty nose with disappointment. "Why would someone kill Uncle Roger...?" She had her thoughts about the matter, but would hold on to those for now, till she got the official read on the investigation.

"I was hoping you could shed more light on that," Dylan said tentatively. "I realize that this is a bad time—the absolute worst—but the more we know and the quicker we know it, the more we have to work with in apprehending the killer as soon as possible." He paused. "I understand that you were video chatting with Roger when the incident occurred...?"

Incident? That almost made it sound like a slight disagreement between neighbors. Or perhaps a confrontation at school that went nowhere. This was no incident, but rather a horrid act of brutality.

Naomi nodded with a heavy sigh, then ran a small hand through her long brunette hair, styled in a shaggy fringe. "We talked mostly about me," she admitted, before the hard part came. "He was always checking up on me, seeing what I was up to. If I needed anything. It was our way of staying connected…" She swallowed and her lower lip shook. "Then he started to talk about the Violet Killer and a lead he'd developed on the person."

Devon pursed his lips. "Did he give you the name of a suspect?"

"Never got the chance before…" The words stuck in her throat like a chicken bone and Naomi forced herself to keep from crying again, needing to be strong to get through this.

"Did Roger happen to send you any information he'd gathered on the case?"

"No. He said he wanted to keep me out of it for the most part." Naomi now wished he had been more forthcoming and she had pressed for more—maybe it might have made a difference—before it was too late. She peered at Dylan's face on the small screen, sensing he was holding something back. What was he not saying? "Why do you ask?"

Dylan scratched his jaw. "Roger's laptop is missing. We think that whoever killed him took it, along with any possible damaging evidence it may have held."

She batted her curly lashes before narrowing her eyes at him. "So, you believe my uncle was the victim of the Violet Killer?"

"Too early to say," Dylan contended ambiguously.

"At this point, we're keeping all options on the table as we investigate what happened."

Reading between the not-so-thick lines, Naomi concluded in her own mind that this serial killer was the key suspect—if not the only one. Especially when coupled with her uncle's cryptic final words. It sent a chill down her spine.

"So, I assume you're coming to the funeral?" Dylan asked, smoothing one of his thick brows.

"Do you even have to ask?" Her eyes grew hotly. "Uncle Roger was the only family I had left…"

"I know." Dylan's shoulders slumped. "Okay, it was a dumb question. Guess I just figured that maybe with your work schedule, it wouldn't permit you the time to break away."

"Seriously?" Her lower lip hung incredulously as he seemed to be digging himself an even deeper tunnel. Was this his way of knocking the Secret Service? Or her for leaving Pebble Creek and him behind? Neither set well with her at the moment. This wasn't about her or them. "I think I'm allowed to attend funerals of loved ones," she said tartly. "Of course I'm coming to Uncle Roger's funeral!"

"Understood." Dylan's voice dropped an apologetic octave. "Let me know when your flight is scheduled to arrive and I can pick you up at the airport."

"Don't do me any favors," she tossed at him sarcastically, still feeling insulted by his insinuation regarding her work and ability to get away. "I'll take an Uber, thank you."

He jutted his chin. "Have it your way."

"I have to go," Naomi said hurriedly, before either said anything else they might regret. Or had they already said pretty much all there was to say of consequence?

"Fine." He lowered a hard gaze, then looked up again, where it seemed to soften. "See you when you get here, unless we somehow manage to avoid each other until the funeral."

She refused to let him bait her into a cynical response. Or did he not want to see her during the trip, as if the memories of what they once had were too painful to separate the man from the detective? If that was the way he felt, far be it for her to object. "Goodbye, Dylan," she said curtly, and hung up.

Afterward, Naomi had second thoughts about the way the call had ended. It was unavoidable that they would cross paths, over and beyond his attendance at the funeral as her uncle's friend and former partner, apart from anything else. In spite of their history, that was then and this was now. Both she and Dylan needed to get past it and act like adults moving forward. At least she intended to, while throwing the ball back squarely into his court.

Naomi went into the peninsula kitchen and poured herself a calming glass of red wine, taking a sip. Admittedly, no matter how adult-like she wanted to handle things with Dylan, she was not looking forward to coming face-to-face again with the man whose heart she broke for all the right reasons. They were certainly right for her at the time, if not him, and she fully understood this. But she saw little chance of dodging Dylan Hester, since he was investigating her uncle's murder and she needed to pay her final respects to him. And there was more to it than that. She had to stick around long enough to make sure that her uncle Roger's killer was brought to justice. Even if that meant bumping heads with her ex. She would just have to deal with any—or all—awkward moments between them as best as possible. Even then, Naomi knew that, where it concerned Dylan, that was much easier said than done.

Chapter Two

Having taken a connecting flight from Portland, Oregon, to Pebble Creek's small but busy airport, Naomi sat in the rear of the Uber, where she took in the sights of the coastal town she grew up in. Not much had changed since her last visit. They passed by cottonwood tree–lined streets with clusters of condominiums, single-family dwellings, small businesses and parks situated throughout. Beyond that were log cabins and farmhouses on rolling hills and forested land. She remembered feeling trapped here, as if the bigger world would somehow pass her by had she not seized the moment when opportunity knocked. How might things have been had she failed to answer the call to improve her life? Would she have forever regretted it? Or gone on a different path where romance and a promising relationship were given a chance to flourish?

Naomi caught a glimpse of the lake where she and Dylan first made love on his friend's boat. The moment was forever etched in her mind, set in stone, and was probably when she realized she had fallen in love with him. It was an experience that shook her entire foundation and made all things seem possible. The truth was, she had never fallen out of love with Dylan. How could what they had have been so easily replaced with another? Yes, she had tried to move on in the romance department, but hadn't had much luck there, not too surprisingly, as Dylan was a hard act to follow. Given the way things ended between them, Naomi was sure Dylan had found someone else to share his life with and couldn't blame him one bit—even if her uncle had suggested otherwise, giving her hope that there might still be a possibility for them to resume their relationship at some point. But she was a realist. After all, she had never given Dylan any indication that there was any hope of them getting back together. How could she and be fair to him? Or herself?

Maybe that was her mistake. Or maybe this was the way it was meant to be.

The car pulled up in front of the two-story Craftsman-style home on Maple Lane that Naomi had grown up in and always saw as a place to come back to. No matter how far away she went.

"Here we are," said the friendly male driver, peering through the rearview mirror.

She acknowledged as much, before getting out. As she stepped into the mid-August sunlight, the hot air hit Naomi in the face like a gentle slap, without the humidity she had grown used to in Miami. After the tall, sandy-haired driver unloaded her bags from the trunk, she thanked him, having tipped in advance.

"Enjoy your stay," he said routinely.

Naomi gave a slight smile, though recognizing that this was anything but a trip to enjoy in returning to her hometown. She carried her travel bags up the cobblestone walkway, almost expecting her beloved uncle Roger to come out and greet her with a big bear hug, as was his custom. The thought that this would never happen again tugged at her heart emotionally.

For an instant, Naomi froze in her tracks, feeling as though someone were watching her through an upstairs ornamental window. Was she imagining things? Or had someone broken in, trying to take advantage of the tragedy, and was caught in the act? After peering at the window again and seeing no one, she quickly dismissed this as the jitters of coming to a now-empty house that sat on two acres of land and overlooked a creek. Stepping onto the front porch with its tapered columns, she took the key out of her hobo bag and unlocked the door.

Inside, Naomi set her bags down and took in the stucco walls, rustic log furniture and parquet flooring. There were a few framed photographs on a living room wall of her uncle standing tall and proud as a detective with the Pebble Creek Police Department and alongside other officers. She moved up to the stone fireplace mantel, where there were photographs of her, Naomi's parents and Roger in happier times. One picture, in particular, caught her eye. It was of Dylan and her, taken by Naomi's uncle while they were at a county fair three years ago. She was surprised he'd kept the photo on display. Or maybe not, considering how fond he was of Dylan, who was like a son to him in every sense of the word. Naomi knew the feeling was mutual, meaning Dylan was probably struggling just as much as she was with her uncle's untimely and violent death in spite of Dylan's loyalty to his job as a detective with the Pebble Creek PD, which needed to come first as he looked into the homicide. Naomi choked back tears as the image of her uncle being gunned down once again flashed in her head. Shaking it off, she walked through the house, soaking up more pleasant memories and reacquainting herself with the surroundings. In the kitchen, dirty dishes were still on the quartz countertop and in the farmhouse sink. Her uncle had never been the tidiest person. Now, sadly, it would be up to her to clean up for him, as though he would eventually come through the front door and thank.

Naomi grabbed her laptop shoulder bag and a garment bag and headed up the squeaky L-shaped stairs. Bypassing the master suite, she stepped inside the spacious bedroom that had once been hers and that Uncle Roger had insisted would always be there any time she wanted to visit. It was taupe colored with a platform bed and pine dresser. A glass computer desk and ergonomic stool sat in the corner. She set up her laptop there, unpacked a few things and took a long shower, feeling lethargic after the long plane ride.

After putting on a fresh set of clothes—a yellow, white-striped top with cuffed sleeves, black straight-legged slacks—she pulled back her thick hair and tied it into a ponytail, applied a tiny amount of makeup, for effect, then slid her feet into a pair of loafers. Naomi headed back downstairs while checking her cell phone for messages. She half expected one might be from Dylan, making sure she had arrived safely. Not that she needed a polite gesture for old times' sake from an ex-boyfriend who had likely moved on to someone else. As it was, there was no call or message from him. Probably just as well, she thought, even if a part of her felt just the slightest—or maybe more than that—disappointment, for whatever reason.

There was, however, a text from her boss, Jared Falcony, the hard-nosed US Secret Service special agent in charge of the Miami Field Office. Though she had taken a few personal days off, Naomi had learned since working for the Secret Service that everyone had to be ready at any time to assume an official capacity in the event of an emergency. But he only wanted to reiterate his condolences for her loss and allow her the time needed to do what she must to get her uncle's affairs in order. She texted back, thanking him.

There was a voice mail from her Secret Service colleague and roommate, Sophia, who specialized in computer and telecommunications fraud investigations. Naomi listened as Sophia offered any help she needed, then updated her on the latest in-house gossip. Nothing out of the ordinary or otherwise to be concerned about.

Naomi was just about to shut off the phone, when

a text message appeared. It came from a caller identified as Blue Violet. The message read simply:

I see you.

Her heart skipped a beat. A Peeping Tom? Or worse, a serial killer? Naomi's heart skipped another beat and her eyes darted around the living area as if someone were actually standing there watching her. She saw no one. Could the person be hiding somewhere, waiting to spring out at her like a ravenous leopard? Feeling panicked, she swiftly moved toward the piece of luggage near the door that contained her department-issued firearm. Unzipping the bag, she removed a locked hard-sided container and managed to steady her trembling hands enough to unlock it. She pulled out a Glock 9-millimeter pistol and a loaded magazine, bringing them together to form a usable weapon of self-defense in this instance.

Crouching low, Naomi moved toward the clerestory windows and peeked through a sliver in the faux wood blinds. There was no indication of anyone surveying the house. Or her. Not that she could see the entire landscape and places one could be hiding atop one of several hills. Or amid the tall cottonwoods and cherry trees on the property. But there was still the possibility that an intruder was inside the house, though Naomi was certain she had locked the front door. Could a window have been left open by Uncle Roger to let fresh air in? And, unknowingly, a dangerous killer?

Determined to maintain her cool under fire, even while potentially in harm's way, Naomi methodically checked each room downstairs, keeping the gun aimed and ready to fire at a moment's notice. She made her way back upstairs and did the same thing, fearful that someone could come out of nowhere and attack. But again, she came up empty. Maybe it was a prankster who had somehow stumbled onto her cell number. Or even a wrong number that came at the wrong time.

While still keeping the firearm handy, Naomi slowly descended the stairs and, thinking she heard a sound, moved cautiously toward the front door. She sensed someone—perhaps her uncle Roger's shooter—was on the other side, hoping to catch her off guard. Not a chance. After sucking in a deep breath, she quietly unlocked and gripped the brass knob, before slowly turning it.

Yanking the door open, she stepped back and aimed the barrel straight at the tall and physically imposing killer's face, while yelling, "Don't move!" Or so she'd imagined the dark-haired, gray-eyed man standing there was the killer.

Naomi reconsidered this belief and gulped when she stared up at the good-looking, square-jawed face and dimpled chin of Dylan Robert Hester.

Though clearly startled, he didn't make a move. Broad shoulders were covered with a navy knit blazer worn over a solid-fitting light pink shirt, and the rest of his well-developed frame filled out nicely in dark blue twill pants. He kept black apron-toe leather shoes firmly in place on the wooden porch.

With a straight look, in a crisp tone of voice, he said coolly, "Welcome back to Pebble Creek, Naomi."

HONESTLY, DYLAN HAD expected a less-than-enthusiastic greeting from the woman he had never quite been able to extricate from his mind, as if meant to forever haunt him with all she brought to the table. Indeed, had she told him to get lost or please don't try to re-create a past she had no interest in resuming, he would have completely understood. After all, her intentions had been pretty clear two years ago where they were concerned. What he hadn't expected was to be treated like an enemy combatant. Especially under the circumstances where they were on the same page, insofar as mourning Roger's death as a homicide. Dylan stared into the barrel of the gun she still had pointed at him, as though in a trance. What was that all about? Had the stress of what happened to her uncle been that much to stomach? "Hello to you, too," he said sardonically. He raised his hands in a mock surrender. "Okay, you've got me. Now would you mind putting that damned thing down, Secret Service Special Agent Lincoln, before someone—me—gets hurt…or worse…?"

Naomi's diamond-shaped face was even lovelier than before, if that was possible. And her tall and slender frame, with long and shapely legs, still left her about six inches shorter than his height of six-three. He liked the ponytail but hoped to get the chance to see her long hair flowing freely while in town, which in his mind enhanced her natural features. Her eyes, an enticing mixture of brown, gold and green hues, locked with his for a long moment as if still assessing her next move. Or target.

"Sorry." She finally lowered the gun while still clutching it tightly. "Thought you were someone else."

"For his sake, I hope the man keeps his distance," Dylan couldn't help but quip, though she had obviously been shaken by someone. Who?

Naomi regarded him suspiciously. "How did you know I was here?" He noticed she was less defensive in her tone, but no less cautious.

"I didn't," he admitted. "I dropped by hoping you would have arrived safe and sound." He grinned sidelong. "Looks like you were ready and waiting..."

"It's not what you think." She glanced at the gun and back. "Didn't want to shoot you." A soft smile played on her thin lips. "Not this time anyway—"

"So you say." He met her eyes dubiously. "Are you going to invite me in?" Naomi seemed to ponder the notion for a long moment, before finally nodding. She stepped aside as Dylan walked past her. When she closed the door and faced him, he had to ask, "What's with the gun? Who did you think was on the other side of the door?"

"I'm not sure..." She walked over to her bag and put the weapon away, replacing it with her cell phone. "Someone calling himself Blue Violet sent me a text." She showed it to Dylan.

"'I see you.'" He read the disturbing words aloud. Even more alarming to him was the sender's handle, Blue Violet. Though this wasn't generally known to the public, it was a moniker that had occasionally been used by the Violet Killer when taunting the police. The perp always used a disposable burner phone for cryptic messages, making it all but impossible for police to track and identify the caller. Was this their serial killer? And why did he send Naomi, of all people, a text?

"I wasn't sure if it was some creep's idea of a sick joke," she said warily. "A voyeur hiding in the woods. Someone who latched onto me randomly and is not watching at all, but getting a charge out of keeping me wondering." Her lower lip quivered. "Or something more sinister, such as this Violet Killer coming after me, like he must have come after Uncle Roger. Either way, it spooked me. Then I heard someone at the door…and, well, I thought I might need to defend myself—"

"I understand." Dylan was glad to know she was well equipped and clearly capable of protecting herself from a dangerous perpetrator. He was less comfortable with the notion that she may have unknowingly made herself a target by returning to Pebble Creek. "You did the right thing."

Naomi peered. "You don't think it was just a prank, do you?"

"No," Dylan told her candidly, not wanting her to let her guard down by sugarcoating it.

She arched an eyebrow. "What aren't you telling me…?"

Normally, he acted on a need-to-know basis during a criminal investigation. But in this case, with the victim being her beloved uncle and her own life at risk, Dylan didn't see any way around it other than being straight with Naomi. He looked at her worriedly. "The man we believe to be the Violet Killer has been known to use Blue Violet as his handle when harassing investigators. He typically tosses the phone after leaving an enigmatic or mocking message."

"But how would he have gotten my cell phone number that's unlisted?" she questioned, ill at ease.

"Roger's cell phone is missing. We think it was taken by the killer, along with his laptop. The unsub would've had access to your cell number and any other personal information stored on the two devices."

Naomi rolled her eyes but remained mute as if waiting for what came next.

Dylan drew a breath, wishing he didn't have to feed her hunger for pertinent information. But the circumstances left him no choice. "Afraid there's more to it than that…"

Her lashes fluttered nervously. "Such as?"

"A violet was found stuffed inside Roger's mouth," Dylan uttered painfully. He shifted his weight from his right foot to the left. "It's the perp's calling card. Meaning that your uncle was, in fact, targeted by this serial killer—most likely because Roger had made it his mission to bring him down and was zeroing in on a suspect."

Naomi sighed. "I believe Uncle Roger was about

to tell me more about the killer when he was silenced…" she spoke bitterly.

"Looks that way." Dylan hated that she had been forced into this investigation, but there was no getting around it. The killer clearly knew who she was and apparently where.

"So, what does he want with me?" Naomi's eyes widened disquietingly. "Or do I even need to ask, given the young women of a similar profile he's gone after…?"

"Maybe nothing," Dylan suggested, even if he suspected otherwise. But tossing at her the worst-case scenario could do more harm than good. Better not to scare her to death for the time being. "Could be that this is just part of the unsub's sick games, meant to scare you and keep us guessing while we track down any leads in the investigation." In truth, Dylan instinctively was troubled by this unexpected twist in the case. Like it or not, so long as she was in town, Naomi had a giant target on her back. Which meant he had to do double duty in both protecting the former love of his life—whether she wanted this or not and in spite of essentially kicking him to the curb two years ago—and capturing a ruthless killer who seemed as confident in his scheming as he was reckless. Dylan hoped that it was the latter that would prove to be the unsub's undoing.

Chapter Three

"What do you think you're doing?" Naomi asked as Dylan moved his large hand toward her face. The last thing she wanted was to give him the idea that this more-than-a-little-awkward reunion between them was step one in getting back together. Not that the notion was unappealing to her on the whole, having thought about what they once had many times and how nice it would be if things had gone in a different direction in their lives. But why start something neither of them was prepared to finish? For better or worse, her life was in Miami now, even if she missed him much more than she cared to admit.

"Just doing you a little favor." He pushed away a tendril of hair that had found its way out of Naomi's gathered hair and fallen across her forehead. His deft finger burned against her tender skin, reminding Naomi of what it felt like when he touched her. "That better?"

"Yes, thank you," she confessed, resisting the urge to scratch where the hair had been.

"Good." He flashed her his trademark crooked

grin that always seemed to win her over. "Now, where were we?"

Naomi found herself weak in the knees as she took in Dylan, who was every bit as nice on the eyes as the day she walked away from him and what they had. The slate-gray eyes were as deeply sexy and mesmerizing as ever. She zeroed in on the cleft in his chin that had always captivated her all by itself. She fought an urge to touch it, hoping he wasn't somehow able to read her mind.

Naomi forced herself to refocus on the moment at hand, freaked out at the thought that a killer had invaded her sense of security and was out there somewhere waiting to strike again. With her as a potential target, so long as she was in Pebble Creek. "Do you think the perp could have been in this house?" Her eyes went around the room, imagining that he had breached her uncle's property—perhaps right under his nose—before turning back to Dylan.

His brows twitched. "Was there any sign of forced entry?"

"No, not that I could detect." But had she been thorough in checking every possible point of access? Maybe she missed something. Wasn't a diabolical killer capable of almost anything, if he put his mind to it?

"I doubt the unsub has been that brazen as to break into Roger's house," Dylan said, rubbing his chin. "Not that I would put it past him, if he was desperate enough—such as believing Roger had kept incriminating information in the house."

"I haven't seen any sign that he brought his work home," she pointed out. Which wasn't exactly the same thing as saying that hadn't been the case.

Dylan chewed his lip. "I didn't get that impression. But still—"

Naomi watched as he scanned the place and could read his mind. "Though Uncle Roger talked about doing it, I see that he never got around to installing a security system, believing the property's location and surroundings to be safe enough to put it off."

"Yeah, I got on him about that." Dylan frowned. "Nowhere in Pebble Creek is safe enough these days, I'm afraid. That notwithstanding, chances are the killer got what and who he was after in Roger's office—and isn't gutsy enough to press his luck by breaking into an ex-cop's house as well, knowing we're in hot pursuit. But that doesn't make the threat any less serious. To be on the prudent side, I'll have a forensics team dust for prints and run a sweep for any hidden cameras or obvious gaps in security."

"Thanks." Naomi appreciated his help to ease her concern, even if Dylan was only doing his job and what came natural as a detective. She supposed it was more than that, given his loyalty toward her uncle. And, if honest about it, Naomi decided that with her past involvement with Dylan, he wouldn't want to see her hurt, in spite of the way things ended between them. Her mind turned to Uncle Roger. Growing up, Naomi had always believed him to be tough as nails, practically invulnerable. Now she knew he had proved to be all too vulnerable against a determined foe who wanted him dead and made it happen.

"In the meantime, I don't think it's a good idea for you to stay here," Dylan cut into her thoughts. He fixed his gaze upon her as if it was more than a mere suggestion.

"I'm sure I'll be fine," she said bravely, even if feeling less than confident on that front. "As you suggested, the killer isn't likely to show his face around here—regardless if I may have overreacted earlier. I just got here and am not about to let him or anyone else drive me away like a frightened little rabbit needing to run for cover."

Dylan, who had made himself comfortable by taking a seat in her uncle's favorite log rocking recliner, gave her a reproving look. "No one, least of all me, is doubting your capabilities and you're certainly much more than a frightened little rabbit. Be that as it may, I still think it's best to err on the side of caution."

Naomi put her resistance on hold for a moment. "How cautious are we talking about?"

"Maybe you could stay at a hotel or—" Dylan stopped on a dime, leaving Naomi to read between the lines.

"With you?" Her eyes widened at the implication, as though it was the worst possible thing he could suggest. She warmed in imagining them living together—even if only temporarily. It was something they had once talked about, when dating seriously as a prelude to getting married. But the proposal never came. Had he gotten cold feet, in spite of hinting at such? She wondered if it would have made a difference if he had asked her to marry him. Would she have said yes and dashed her plans to work for the Secret Service?

"Hadn't meant to suggest anything of the sort," he claimed smoothly. "It's not a half-hearted come-on, I promise. We've been over and done with for two years now. I get that. It is what it is. That said, I do have plenty of room and a guest bedroom at my house. It's by the lake, has a nice security system and isn't likely to attract unwanted visitors. I would be happy to play host during your stay in town. I just want you to be safe, Naomi. I owe that much to Roger."

Though she found his offer more than a little tempting, Naomi gave him a firm, "Thanks but no thanks, Dylan. I'm a member of the US Secret Service, more than capable of protecting myself from any threat that comes my way. If the person who killed my uncle wants to come after me, too, he is welcome to try. I have my gun and know how to use it. I'm also trained in hand-to-hand combat and jujitsu. So, I'm not going anywhere." Naomi sighed, while trying hard not to show him that in spite of everything she just said, having a demented serial killer possibly set his sights on her was still very unsettling. To say the least.

"Well, you've made your case admirably," Dylan said, his voice spiced with sarcasm and resignation. "As you already seem to have your mind made up in the stubborn tradition of your uncle, I won't persist in trying to dissuade you from staying."

Naomi smiled thinly. "In following Uncle Roger's footsteps, I'll take that as a badge of honor," she said proudly.

"It is," he agreed and got to his feet. "Just be careful."

"I will be." She knew his concern for her welfare was genuine. As was hers for his health and well-being, the awkwardness of the moment to go with their estrangement as a couple notwithstanding.

Dylan stepped closer. "Do you need any help with the arrangements, now that Roger's body has been released to the funeral home?"

Truthfully, Naomi had barely wrapped her head around the idea that her uncle was dead and, as his only living relative, she would need to step up and see to it that he had a proper burial. But that wouldn't stop her from doing what needed to be done. "I think I can handle it," she responded placidly. "Uncle Roger purchased a burial plot right next to my parents' resting place in the cemetery. He wanted to be buried beside his brother, whom he was very close to."

"Okay." Dylan nodded thoughtfully. "I have to go. If you run into any problems along the way, you have my number."

"I'll keep that in mind," she promised, feeling the warmth from their close proximity. She took an involuntary step backward lest she allow a desire to touch him cloud her judgment that it was best to leave the past where it was. "Please keep me abreast on the investigation into Uncle Roger's death."

"I will." He put his hands together. "Roger's SUV

should be released shortly, after forensics is finished combing it for possible evidence pertaining to the crime. I'm sure he'd want you to have it—so long as you need transportation while you're in town."

"Thank you." Naomi imagined it would feel weird driving her uncle's SUV, knowing he would never be behind the wheel himself again. It was just another adjustment she would need to make, difficult as it was.

Dylan glanced over at the bag where she had placed her firearm and grinned out of the side of his mouth. "I'm guessing you finished at the head of your class among Secret Service agents in firearms training?"

"Close enough," Naomi admitted, actually taking second place, just behind her friend Sophia. "It's an ongoing process throughout every agent's career with the Service."

"Figured as much, as it's the same for those of us in the Pebble Creek PD."

She gazed at him in earnest. "I really wouldn't have shot you, if that's what you're thinking." She hoped he knew deep down inside that she would always care for him enough to stay out of harm's way, including bullet wounds.

"Nice to know." He held her gaze with a straight look. "The last thing I need is to be mistaken for the bad guy where you're concerned."

"You were never the bad guy, Dylan." She wanted to make this clear to him. "My leaving wasn't about you." She thought he understood that. Or had this just been wishful thinking on her part?

"I know—that's what you told me." Skepticism rang from his tenor.

"It was true." Her voice did not waver. The last thing Naomi ever wanted was for him to think that their breakup was a reflection of her no longer wanting them to be together. Couldn't have been further from the truth. In an ideal world, they both could have had it all, beginning with each other. But in this real world, she was forced to choose one path over another, painful as it was. So she did, knowing she would have to live with the consequences, for richer or poorer. Sickness or health. Love or loss.

"I just wish we had talked about it more," Dylan asserted, as if still carrying a mighty chip on his broad shoulder.

Naomi winced, wishing they didn't have to deal with this now. What more was there to say? Would it have made any difference had he asked her to stay? Had she needed to hear those powerful words come out of his mouth? No matter. It was too late now for what never happened. Wasn't it?

"There's no point in going there, Dylan," Naomi argued, fighting off the feelings of guilt that gnawed at her like a final exam she needed to pass or risk failure.

His jaw clenched. "I get it, you've moved on."

"Haven't you?" she assumed pensively in meeting his hard eyes.

Dylan shifted his gaze and took a deep breath before returning to her face. "Yeah, I guess I have."

Had she expected him to say otherwise when giving him no reason not to move on with his life? She wondered miserably what his current girlfriend looked like. Gorgeous, Naomi supposed. Probably sexy, too. She'd never asked her uncle specifically about Dylan's personal life, not sure she wanted to know.

The idea of another woman stealing Dylan's heart, soul and bed bothered Naomi more than she'd realized. Till now.

THROUGH HIGH-POWERED BINOCULARS, the Violet Killer watched inconspicuously from a safe distance atop an uneven hill, behind a cluster of large ferns. He saw the dark-haired, tall police detective step outside the house with the striking niece of Roger Lincoln. She looked even better than he remembered. And better than the images Lincoln had of her on his computer, which was now in the possession of the Violet Killer. Along with incriminating information that could have exposed him to the local authorities and FBI agents trying to track him down like a wild animal on the loose. He sensed the overprotectiveness of Detective Dylan Hester as though he was determined not to let her slip from his grasp and into the arms of a killer. But the detective's efforts would prove futile. As they had with the others the Violet Killer had set his sights on. Now that Lincoln's niece had become the latest object of his affections—and long overdue at that—the Violet Killer intended to settle for nothing less than to see to it that Naomi Lincoln joined his other violets in blissful death.

But all in good time. Fortunately, patience had been his virtue for the past two years, serving him well when he needed it most, against his worst instincts. He wasn't about to get too overeager or cocky to his own detriment. Not when half the fun was watching and waiting like a lion and its helpless prey, till the perfect time to strike. By then, it would be too late to do anything other than accept her fate. Until then, he would continue to hide in plain view, loving the attention he was getting and the satisfying fear he had brought upon the citizens of Pebble Creek. Especially the women, many of whom had become afraid of their own shadows.

The Violet Killer gazed through the binoculars as the pretty Secret Service agent headed back into the house and the police detective casually walked away and got into his vehicle. He sat in it for a while as though reluctant to leave, and the killer could only imagine what steps he was taking to try to keep Lincoln's niece out of harm's way. Try all he wished, but it would make no difference when all was said and done. Naomi Lincoln was living on borrowed time before she joined her uncle—who overplayed his hand and paid for it—in the grave.

The Violet Killer furtively stepped away from the bushes and coolly made his way down the other side of the hill and to his own car. Inside, he started it and was on his merry way, while making plans as he usually did in staying one step ahead of everyone else.

Chapter Four

Dylan sat in his car for a long moment outside Roger's house, regretting that he had let things get personal with Naomi. He had no right to act like a bitter ex, even if part of him felt that way. He hadn't exactly fought hard to keep her there in Pebble Creek, thinking it best not to stand in the way of a dream she worked hard to achieve. Never mind if it came at the expense of asking her to marry him and all that might have occurred afterward as husband and wife. Not to mention father and mother, had they decided to go in that direction. But that was two years ago and their beds had been made. Right now, he needed to stay focused and give Naomi what she really needed from him: capturing the man who murdered her uncle. This, of course, would achieve the added goal of stopping the Violet Killer in his tracks, hopefully before any more young women could be lost. Including Naomi herself, who Dylan believed was a potential target for the killer.

After starting the car, Dylan drove off. He got on the speaker of his cell phone and ordered investigators to come to Roger's house with Naomi's consent to dust for fingerprints that might not belong and other possible indicators that it was part of the homicide that took place at Roger's office—including running a sweep for any illegal surveillance or audio equipment. With that in motion, Dylan rang Detective Gregory Hwang.

"Is Naomi here?" he asked curiously.

"Yeah. Just left her at Roger's house," Dylan informed him, wishing they could have spent more time talking, against his better judgment.

"How's she holding up?"

"About as well as you might expect when you're a virtual eyewitness to your only living relative being gunned down."

"Yeah, figured as much," grumbled Hwang.

Dylan concurred, feeling helpless at the thought of losing his good friend. "What did you come up with on the security cameras inside or outside Roger's building?"

"Not much we can use, I'm afraid. A camera inside wasn't working and one outside showed movement around the time in question, but so far everyone we've been able to identify checked out as far as what they were doing there and when. We've extended the perimeter in checking out other surveillance cameras in the area that might have picked up something."

"Good." Dylan sighed, sensing that the killer was too clever to make himself easy to pick out of the crowd, much less identify, without some effort. Especially given his almost uncanny ability to go after young women with near impunity. "Naomi got a text message from Blue Violet, claiming he was watching her. Must have homed in on her after stealing Roger's cell phone."

"You think he's actually going after Naomi next…?" Hwang's voice dropped an unnerved octave.

"At this point, I wouldn't put anything past the unsub," admitted Dylan, wishing he could feel otherwise. "What better way to really get under our skin than targeting Naomi as another way to show his total disregard for the law, while challenging us to stop him?"

"Are you planning to let Naomi stay with you while in town, to be on the safe side?" Hwang asked curiously.

It was a reasonable question that Dylan would have expected from the detective, who knew that his fondness for Naomi had never wavered, their differences aside. And that protecting her from a madman was a priority. Too bad she couldn't see it that way at the moment. "Right now, she wants to stay put," he said, acquiescing to this. "For the time being, I'd like to beef up patrols in the area and keep tabs on her."

"I'll put in the request," Hwang agreed. "Shouldn't be a problem."

"Hope not." Dylan knew that with the serial killer investigation underway, the department's manpower was being stretched thin. Maybe the perp was counting on this to terrorize Naomi right under their noses. Dylan wasn't about to allow that to happen. Not if he could help it.

After disconnecting, Dylan headed for the Pebble

Creek Police Department crime laboratory, where
the bullet removed from Roger's head had been ana-
lyzed, along with the shell casing found at the scene
of the crime. Dylan saw this as an important step in
trying to identify the unsub, who in an apparent act
of desperation went away from his normal MO in
shooting Roger to death.

Entering the modern lab, Dylan was greeted by
George Suina, a forensic and firearms analyst and
full-blooded Pueblo Indian, who had been with the
department for nearly a decade. His jet-black hair,
just grazing narrow shoulders, belied his midfifties
age. "Hey, Dylan," he said in a friendly tone. "Bet I
know why you're here."

Dylan grinned humorlessly. "You know me too
well, George. What have you got for me?"

"Plenty." His sable eyes widened teasingly. "Come
with me."

Dylan followed him to a workstation, where
Suina had a monitor on, with a split screen overhead.
"Looks like you were spot-on, Dylan, in linking the
bullet casing you found with the bullet taken out of
Roger Lincoln. On the right side of the screen is an
image of the mangled bullet removed from Lincoln's
head," explained Suina. "It was fired from a gun barrel with four lands and grooves and had a left-hand
twist." He turned to the other side of the screen as
Dylan observed attentively an image of a shell casing. "As you suspected, the ballistic markings on
the .45 ACP casing you located are a perfect match

with those from the bullet that killed Roger Lincoln. Or, in other words, both came from the same gun."

Dylan nodded sullenly. "Figured as much. Looks like our serial killer unsub is packing a .45 ACP handgun...and is more dangerous than ever." Not to mention likely being in possession of Roger's Ruger Blackhawk revolver as well. Meaning there was an even greater sense of urgency in bringing him down. "I don't suppose you were able to pull any prints off the bullet or shell casing?"

"No such luck, I'm afraid." Suina shook his head, frowning. "On the fingers-crossed side of things, though, with the good possibility that the shooter used the same weapon before, we've entered the bullet and shell casing evidence into the ATF's National Integrated Ballistic Information Network, with the aim of getting a hit on the firearm and triggerman."

"One can only hope," Dylan said and crossed the fingers on both hands theatrically in support of this effort. Having worked previously with the ATF or Bureau of Alcohol, Tobacco, Firearms and Explosives, he knew they were a great federal partner in the war on crime. Maybe this case would be no exception in achieving results. But he wasn't expecting miracles, either, knowing that the unsub was not going to make this easy for them to bring him down, having proved that after two years of serial murdering. But he had made a tactical error in going after Roger, and it just might be the first step to his undoing.

AFTER DYLAN LEFT, Naomi put aside her unease to finish unpacking. She wondered if it had been a mistake not to take up his offer of refuge. Was she letting her pride get in the way of common sense? On the other hand, wasn't that putting the cart ahead of the horse to allow paranoia to run her out of the house prematurely? Till proven otherwise, she had to assume that her uncle's house—soon to be hers if she read him correctly when alive—was safe enough to go about her business, knowing that she had self-protection, should it come to that.

Just as she was trying to decide what to have for dinner, with the pickings in the refrigerator rather slim, Naomi jumped when she heard the doorbell ring. Her first instinct was to go for her weapon. That thought quickly subsided as she looked out the peephole and recognized one of the three people standing there—one woman and two men—as being Tabitha McKinnon, a crime scene investigator for the Pebble Creek PD from when Naomi did some work for them as a crime victims service coordinator. Dylan had given her a heads-up that they were on their way to dust for prints and check for bugs, but she had spaced out on this with different things on her mind. She noted they were carrying equipment for their assignment.

Naomi opened the door and greeted them with a smile. "Hey, Tabitha." She singled her out, having to look up at the tall, thirtysomething woman with butterscotch-blond hair cut short with curtain bangs.

"Hi, Naomi. Nice to see you again. Sorry it's under these circumstances."

"So am I." Naomi eyed the two men, also in their thirties. One was a tall Hispanic, his dark thick hair worn in a pompadour style. The other was African American, even taller, with a jet-black flat top. Tabitha introduced them as Detective Raymond Cruz and forensic science technician Vince Iverson, respectively.

"Detective Hester asked us to give the place a sweep for bugs and see if we can collect any forensic evidence that points toward an intruder entering the premises," Iverson said.

"Yes, I was expecting you." Naomi invited them in. "Thanks for coming."

"We'll try to be quick, if not thorough," Cruz told her, removing latex gloves from his blazer pocket.

Realizing her presence would only be in their way, possibly delaying doing their jobs, Naomi said, "Why don't I get out of your way. I could use some fresh air anyway. Just holler when you're done."

"Will do." Tabitha smiled at her. "Hopefully, we won't find anything unusual."

Naomi seconded that as she grabbed her cell phone and was out the door. Fortunately, she had put everything away that needed to be. With any luck, the coast would be cleared to make the most of her time there, while feeling relatively safe and secure. She took a deep breath and made her way to the wooded area on the property where she had spent much time when living there, hiking and running on a well-worn path, two of her favorite pastimes. She recalled being joined by Dylan once in a while, though they tended to use the isolation from the house more to make out than exercise. Admittedly, she missed the feel of his mouth upon hers and wondered if it could happen again.

Naomi's reverie was interrupted by the sound of crackling leaves. She nearly jumped out of her skin as she whipped around, thinking she might be attacked and preparing for battle, having left her firearm at the house. But instead of a deadly assailant, she witnessed a rather large brown squirrel with a long tail scurry across dirt and leaves, hop onto a cottonwood tree, climb up like its tail was on fire and leap from one precarious branch to another, till out of sight. Naomi couldn't help but smile, reminding her of what she loved about the Pacific Northwest and its varied inhabitants blending so well with nature.

With the scare behind her, she headed back to the house, figuring they must be nearly through with their work. No sooner had she reached the door than Tabitha stepped onto the porch. "I was just about to come looking for you."

Naomi sensed by her expression that something was up. But what? "Did you find something—?"

"Let's go back inside," Tabitha said evasively.

"Okay." Naomi followed her through the door, where Cruz and Iverson were standing over the rustic coffee table. Several items were spread across it. "What's this?" she asked.

Cruz turned to her with a sour look on his face. "We found a number of bugging devices throughout the house," he said, holding one of them up with a gloved hand. "They include tiny cameras and electronic listening devices. Seems as though someone's been keeping tabs on Roger and his activities, apparently without him being the wiser."

Naomi was shocked. The thought that her uncle's house had been bugged rattled her. Equally unnerving was the notion that someone might have been watching her while naked before and after her shower. "Who could have done such a thing?" she asked, but she already had her suspicions, when coupled with Uncle Roger's death purportedly at the hands of the Violet Killer. Could the two be unrelated?

"We're not sure," Cruz said with a catch to his voice. "Obviously one or more persons on a mission of some sort to monitor Roger—or anyone else coming and going to the house."

"Did you get all the bugs?" Naomi's eyes popped wide with pessimism.

"We think so," Iverson chipped in confidently. "We'll double-check, to be on the safe side."

"The bugs have been dusted for prints and we'll also see if we can pull any DNA off them," Tabitha said. "Maybe we'll get lucky. Same with the other data we've gathered."

Cruz frowned. "Given the circumstances surrounding Lincoln's death and no security system on the premises, my advice to you, Naomi, is to stay elsewhere till this is sorted out, for your own safety."

"I'll keep that in mind," she said tightly, recognizing how vulnerable she was at the house with a serial killer on the loose. She wondered if Dylan was still up for some company. Or would that cramp his style as a single man who had admitted to having one or more women take her place in his life?

DYLAN HAD ALREADY been on his way to Roger's house to see if they had found anything interesting when his cell phone rang. He grabbed it off the car seat and saw the caller was Naomi. A pang of excitement coursed through him to hear the sound of her voice, just as had been the case when they were seeing each other. That dampened somewhat as he came back to reality and the fact that he and she were no longer a couple, hard as this continued to be to come to terms with. He clicked on the speakerphone. "Hey," he said to her equably. "What's up?"

"Does that offer to stay at your place for now still stand?" she asked. He could hear the tension in her tone.

"Of course." He could use the company—her company, in particular. But he wasn't about to say that. Or draw the wrong conclusions again. "Why the change of heart?"

"They found the place bugged!" Naomi snapped. "Someone had been watching and listening to Uncle Roger, for who knows how long..."

Dylan cursed under his breath. He was pretty sure that someone was the Violet Killer. Though this was not the modus operandi of the serial killer, per se, desperate times may have called for desperate measures. Perhaps he had been tracking Roger's movements for some time, as the former police detective had been tracking the unsub and homing in on his identity.

With no security system in place and relatively easy access to the house, it wouldn't have been too difficult for someone to break in and plant the devices, unbeknownst to Roger. Or Naomi, for that matter.

"I'm sure your colleagues will fill you in on the details…" Naomi's bitter voice broke into his thoughts.

Dylan could only hope the installer had been careless and left behind prints, DNA or other evidence they could work with in identifying the perp. Meanwhile, Naomi needed to be protected from whoever might wish to come after her. "Repack your bags. I'm on my way," he said, his voice steadfast.

"I intend to have a security system installed," she pointed out defiantly. "Then I'll be out of your hair in no time."

"You can play in my hair anytime you want." Dylan remembered how much she loved running her hands through his thick hair. And vice versa. Now was probably not the right time to think about that, but he couldn't help himself. "Seriously," he amended, "you needn't be in any hurry to go back there. As I said, my place is more than large enough to accommodate you for as long as you're in town." He assumed that would be for only a few days. After the funeral, he imagined she would be eager to return to the new life she had established for herself. Dylan found himself strangely already starting to wish that weren't true. At the same time, so long as a killer was on the prowl, he believed that the farther away from Pebble Creek Naomi was, the better.

"See you when you get here," she told him without comment, and hung up.

Right after, his cell phone rang again. This time it was Tabitha. "Hey," he told her, while keeping an eye on the road. "Naomi just told me about the bugs found."

"Yeah, looks like someone was up to no good in planting surveillance equipment in Roger's house," she reiterated.

"Why don't you guys do a sweep of his office," Dylan ordered. "Maybe there's something there we missed."

"Sure thing."

"Let me know if you find anything." He had no doubt she would at that, even while Dylan wondered just what the unsub or someone else hoped to get out of such listening and video devices. It did no good to speculate but he would anyway. Information was valuable only when you had possession of it. He wouldn't put it past Roger's killer to use any means necessary to protect his identity, including trying to stay one step ahead. Or keep his opponent one or two steps behind. Whatever it took.

ADMITTEDLY, NAOMI HAD been curious about the house Dylan lived in. When they were together, he was staying in a condominium in the center of town. It was a bit small, but cozy in a manly type of way. Her uncle had mentioned casually last year that Dylan had purchased the lakefront home without giving many details, other than that he was living there alone at the time. Was he still? A flash of jealousy ripped through Naomi at the prospect of another woman stealing Dylan's heart, as if it would always belong to her. How silly was that, all things being equal?

Dylan drove his department-issued vehicle onto a circular drive till they came to a Western red cedar log cabin, two stories high. "Well, this is it," he said nonchalantly. "Home sweet home."

"I see…" was all Naomi could say, noting that aside from the Pebble Creek Lake frontage, the lush landscaping included mature aspen trees for privacy. She could only imagine what the inside looked like.

As though reading her mind, Dylan said with a half grin, "Shall we go in?"

She smiled. "Yes."

They got out of the car and unloaded her bags, before heading up a winding concrete paver walkway and onto a wraparound deck with reclaimed barn oak planks and two wooden Adirondack chairs. Inside the cabin, Naomi stepped on multicolored slate tile flooring. A quick scan showed her cedar wood walls with a vaulted ceiling and exposed beams. The floor-to-ceiling windows had open sheer drapes and looked out majestically onto the lake. Modern minimalist furnishings blended with contemporary accent pieces caught her eye.

"Shall I give you the grand tour?" The deep sound of Dylan's voice reached her as he was turning off the security system.

"I'd love that," she gushed, unable to help herself,

as she had always been intrigued by architectural design in housing.

They set the bags down and proceeded to go through the downstairs, which included a two-story rusticated brickwork fireplace in the great room, a gourmet kitchen with black stainless steel appliances, butcher block countertops and island with wooden swivel stools.

"It's awesome," Naomi admitted.

"Yeah." Dylan seemed to take it in stride.

She gave him a curious look. "So why did you decide to sell your condo?"

"I always talked about wanting something on the lake—or have you forgotten?" He didn't give her a chance to respond, as if to rub it in. "When this place came on the market at a great price, I jumped on it, loving the idea to be right there at the water for swimming, fishing and boating."

Naomi realized that they had talked about living in such a place together. She couldn't help but wonder what might have been if she had stayed and moved in with him. Going up the flight of solid wood spiral stairs and seeing the second floor was no less impressive to Naomi, as each room was spacious with antique furnishings and large bay windows. They lingered just long enough in the master suite with its king sleigh bed that she couldn't help but consider whom he might be sharing the bed with these days. Was it really any of her business at this stage of the game?

Dylan didn't seem to notice her contemplation—

or maybe decided to keep it to himself—as he guided her past a fully furnished room that had been turned into a home office, to the guest bedroom, which was as impressive as the others. It had a panel bed, rustic dresser and a comfortable-looking wingback chair.

"This is yours, for as long as you like," he said evenly. "There's a full bathroom right through that door." He pointed across the room.

"Thank you." Naomi gazed up at him. "Are you sure I'm not imposing?"

"I'm sure."

She should have left it at that, but did not. "I just don't want this to be weird."

"Weird?" He cocked a brow. "How so?"

"Not sure how your current girlfriend would feel having your ex staying at your cabin, even for a few days…"

"Wouldn't know about that, since I don't currently have a girlfriend. So you're safe." Dylan grinned with amusement. "I'll bring up your bags and then whip up something in the kitchen. You must be starving. I know I am."

With that, he left her there and Naomi wondered how she ever let him get away. Her reasons were certainly sound enough. She loved her job, her apartment and the fast-paced lifestyle of Miami. But was it enough in the absence of a meaningful relationship with a significant other? Especially after losing her uncle, the one man who seemed to get her. Other than Dylan.

Chapter Five

While making a fresh salad to go with leftover lemon baked chicken breasts and bran muffins, Dylan couldn't help but imagine him and Naomi cooking meals together in the gourmet kitchen. After all, that had been the plan, right? Till she bailed on him and any future they might have had. Including buying the dream log cabin he now occupied, as husband and wife. But he couldn't and shouldn't hold that against her. Not after two years of trying to put what they had behind him. No, he had to stay focused for the moment on keeping Naomi safe for as long as she let him. At least till they were able to get the jump on the Violet Killer before he could ever lay a hand on her. Or, for that matter, hopefully any other woman who fell into his crosshairs.

"There you are..." Dylan gave a halfhearted smile.

"What can I do?" Naomi asked. He noticed that she had let her hair down. He liked the shaggy fringe hairstyle. It suited her. Dylan imagined his hands could get lost in all that hair.

"You can grab the wine out of the fridge." He paused for effect. "I assume you still like red wine?"

She smiled to one side of her mouth self-consciously. "Yes."

"Good. The wineglasses are in there." He pointed toward the glass-front cabinet, above the double-bowl, drop-in sink.

"Will do." He watched her open and pour the wine, while thinking how sexy she looked in the process, even if not the wiser.

They sat at the natural wood dining table in silence while watching each other eat, before Naomi batted her lashes and asked ill at ease, "You're going to get this guy, right?"

"Yeah, we will," Dylan promised. He could read the uncertainty in her eyes and the pain of loss she had been forced to endure at the hands of a serial killer. This made Dylan all the more determined to make his words hold up. "It's only a matter of time."

"But how many more people have to die before then?" she questioned, while slicing a knife into the chicken breast.

"Wish I could answer that," he spoke honestly, sitting back in his chair. To do otherwise would be disingenuous when dealing with a serial killer, who by his very nature killed more than two people to qualify as such. Meaning any indeterminate number would likely be followed till he could be stopped. "The good news is that we now know the caliber and model of the gun used to shoot Roger. It's an important piece of the puzzle in trying to nail the unsub."

"He probably ditched the weapon." Naomi brushed her nose. "Or stole it to make it harder to trace."

"Maybe—but my guess is that using the firearm was a spontaneous attack that came only after the killer found himself desperate to maintain his anonymity." Dylan wiped his mouth with a paper napkin. "That, along with his arrogance as a serial murderer, tells me that he likely still has the gun— believing he's safe to use it again, if necessary."

Naomi rolled her eyes. "You're probably right. Hope it leads to his downfall." She picked up a muffin and rotated as if inspecting it, then took a small bite and looked at him. "So, how's your mom these days?"

"She's good," he answered stoically, realizing Naomi was deliberately shifting the conversation to something a little more palatable. For his part, talking about his mother was less than ideal, though Naomi got along well with her when his mother chose to be around, which wasn't often. Abigail Sorenson, who used her second husband's surname, left his father when Dylan was just six years old. She had been ambiguous about the reasons why, but he suspected it had to do with his father's alcohol abuse and inability to hold down a job. Even with that knowledge, Dylan had a hard time dealing with the separation to this day, always wondering in the back of his mind if it was something he did or didn't do that was the final straw in the divorce. "My mother's on husband number three now," Dylan uttered with a shrug. "He's the lawyer who handled divorce number two. They're currently living in Vermont."

Naomi met his eyes with an unreadable look. "Do you get out there much to visit?"

"Not much. Too busy these days." He left it at that, while wondering if she would.

"And your sister?" Naomi probed, forking lettuce.

Dylan smiled, finding her a more welcoming topic. "Stefany's doing great." His sister was four years older and an anesthesiologist, working as an infectious disease specialist with Doctors Without Borders, along with her Argentine husband, Theodore Gonzalez. Stefany didn't seem to have the same hang-ups regarding their parents that he did, which Dylan believed was a good thing. "She's currently busy saving lives in Southern Africa," he said satisfyingly.

"That's wonderful." Naomi flashed her teeth. "You must be so proud of her, doing such a noble thing with her life."

"I am, definitely." Dylan sipped his wine, gazing at Naomi. He wondered if she thought any less of her own lot in life as a Secret Service agent. Did he think less of his own career? "Of course, all things are relative," he pointed out coolly. "We all make choices and as long as Stefany is happy with hers, so am I." Even as the words came out of his mouth, Dylan regretted saying them, so as to imply things he didn't necessarily wish to regarding Naomi's career choice.

She seemed to pick up on this. Lifting her glass, she took a quick drink and uttered, while getting to her feet, "Think I'll call it a night, if you don't mind…"

"Hope it wasn't something I said," Dylan voiced lamely.

"It wasn't." Naomi put on a brave face. "I've just had a long day and am exhausted."

"I understand." He kept his voice level and stood, not wanting to make things worse between them. When Naomi was about to remove her plates from the table, he said, "Leave it. You should get some rest. I'll clean up and…see you in the morning."

She nodded and forced a smile. "Good night, Dylan, and thanks again for letting me stay here."

"No problem," he assured her.

"By the way," she said, after taking a few steps, "I assume you can recommend a great security system I can have installed at Uncle Roger's house?"

"Yeah, I can do that."

"Good."

Dylan didn't go any further, watching as she walked away and up the stairs. As it was, he really didn't see the point in putting in a security system in a house that she would presumably be placing on the market with her return to Miami. Unless she planned to hold on to the property as an investment. Or do something to increase its value before selling. Whatever the case, he intended to delay making that recommendation for as long as possible. Or at least till they could get a better handle on the unsub as a legitimate threat to Naomi in Pebble Creek.

After clearing the table and putting the plates, silverware, and glasses into the dishwasher, Dylan grabbed his cell phone and got the latest update on the investigation from some members of the Violet Killer Task Force, while strategizing on where they went from here with a deadly perpetrator still on the hunt to add to his violets and victims.

By the time he had hit the sack an hour later, Dylan found himself unable to sleep. Indeed, sleep had been hard to come by ever since he had been working this case. Even harder since Roger Lincoln was murdered. Beyond that, sleep wasn't coming any easier knowing that Naomi was just down the hall, undoubtedly sleeping like a beautiful baby after her long flight and scary moments at her uncle's house. Dylan had once thought they would be sharing that bed the whole night through, night after night— making love with all the passion and promise that came from being together two years ago. But that dream had died a slow death, replaced by the reality that Naomi had moved on to a different part of the country. With possibly another man in her life.

When Dylan finally drifted off to sleep, that last thought played on his emotions more than he wanted to admit.

NAOMI'S HEART RACED as she watched her uncle Roger gunned down before her very eyes. He slumped over, a wound to his head bleeding profusely. The unsub was just out of sight. But then, his twisted face suddenly appeared, filling the laptop screen. She didn't recognize him. His dark, foreboding eyes stared back at her; then he broke out into maniacal laughter that boomed in her ears. She shrieked, drowning him out and, in the frightful moment, forcing her awake, having broken out in a cold sweat.

It was just a nightmare, Naomi realized, once she had come to terms with the fact that she was in bed, alone, safe from the bad man who murdered her uncle. But whose bed? It took her another moment to regain her equilibrium and remember that she was staying in Dylan's guest room. She half expected him to come rushing in like a good looking knight in shining armor, having heard her cries, as she had when opening her eyes. What would she tell him? It was so embarrassing, even if he understood on some level, given the horror of what she had witnessed two days ago. She could only hope this was a one-off. The last thing she needed was to be haunted by this creep.

Dylan never came in. With the light of day streaming in through the bamboo blinds, she knew that it was daytime. Grabbing her cell phone from beneath the plush pillow, Naomi saw that it was just after 7:00 a.m. She had been so tired that she slept through the night. Before that, she recalled feeling the sting in Dylan's unfavorably comparing her career choice with his sister, Stefany's. Or had she only imagined something that was totally off base? Either way, it hadn't set well with Naomi. She didn't need to be reminded of what—or who—she gave up. There was no pushing a rewind button. Surely he knew that. So why insinuate what might have been had she chosen to stay in Pebble Creek? With him?

Dragging herself up, Naomi pushed aside the thoughts, wanting only to get through the funeral and back to the life she had created in Miami. But could it possibly be that easy to leave and forget everything and everyone who had brought her back home? Including, on at least some level, Dylan Hester?

After washing up and putting on clothes, Naomi went downstairs, expecting that Dylan may have made her breakfast, in playing the role of host. Instead, she found a note he'd left on the kitchen counter and started reading it:

Morning, Sleepyhead—hope you slept well. Had to go to work. There's coffee made. The fridge is stocked and a couple of cereals are in the cabinet. Help yourself to whatever you like. I had someone drive Roger's SUV over, which I'm guessing you'll need. Keys are inside. If you need anything else, let me know. See you later. Dylan.

He added the four-digit master code to the alarm system for turning it off and on as needed.

Naomi smiled. Looked as if he'd thought of everything. Though part of her felt she could get used to this—including his comfortable cabin and the man himself—the other part of her felt that might be a big mistake that neither of them needed. Right now, she only wanted to get some coffee into her system and a bite to eat, and then continue the difficult task of funeral preparations for her uncle Roger.

Forty-five minutes later, Naomi was inside his red Ford Explorer. She picked up the familiar scent of her uncle, making it all the more difficult to know that he was gone and wasn't coming back, no matter how much she wanted to convince herself other-

wise. She could only hope that his killer was made
to pay for what he'd done, sooner than later, through
arrest, conviction, and incarceration.

Naomi drove down the winding road away from
Dylan's cabin, wondering how long she would stay
there. Would he really be okay with them temporarily sharing the same space and separate bedrooms?
Would she? Thoughts of when they were red-hot lovers
crossed her mind, causing a bodily reaction. She managed to still the heated waters of desire that had never
gone away for the man, even with thousands of miles
separating them. Was it as difficult for him as well, putting aside the bitter feelings that were likely still per-
meating on his part? Just because he wasn't currently
involved with anyone didn't mean he was a monk, either. Even if that thought irritated her, Naomi had to
draw the line on natural jealousy and being reasonable,
given their situations as they were. Not like she had any
other choice in the matter.

Gazing up at the rearview mirror, she noticed a
dark SUV on her tail, seemingly coming out of nowhere. She couldn't see the face of the driver through
tinted glass. Was he or she doing that deliberately?
Naomi pressed down on the accelerator, increasing
her speed, putting some distance between her and the
other vehicle. Just as she thought she was safe, it came
upon her again, so close that she feared the driver
might ram into her and try to force her off the road.
What was their problem? Naomi's pulse raced as she
envisioned the driver being none other than the Violet Killer—the man Dylan believed was responsible

for her uncle's death. Was he coming after her now? But how would he have known her whereabouts? Unless he had followed them from her uncle's house yesterday and waited patiently for a chance to strike.

Again, Naomi sped up, her heart beating wildly. Just as she was prepared to dart into an upcoming strip mall parking lot, believing it might be her best chance to survive, having left her gun packed away, the SUV mysteriously stopped the aggressive tactics. It actually had slowed down and turned onto a side street and quickly disappeared from view, making Naomi wonder if she had imagined the whole thing. Maybe this serial killer thing was getting to her in ways that had her questioning her judgment when she needed to remain in control. Or might that have been the unsub's plan all along, to keep her guessing and off balance?

She drove into the strip mall parking lot and, after pulling into an open slot, sucked in a deep, calming breath. Taking out her cell phone, Naomi rang her best friend with the Secret Service, Sophia Menendez, for a video chat, needing to hear a familiar voice. She accepted the request, her gorgeous face appearing on the screen, surrounded by a brown ombre hairstyle with bangs. Bold, dark eyes stared at Naomi.

"You look like you've seen a ghost!" Sophia said, never one to mince words.

"Not quite, but something just as unsettling." Naomi made a face. "Or at least in my, at times, vivid imagination."

"Tell me…" her friend pressed.

"I could've sworn that a dark-colored SUV was trying to run me off the road—or worse." Naomi gasped.

"What would give you that idea?"

"It started with a text message I got when I arrived at my uncle's house," she told her, "from someone calling himself Blue Violet."

"As in the Violet Killer?" Sophia's full lower lip hung down. As a true crime addict, she was fascinated with the case before Naomi ever mentioned her uncle Roger's involvement.

"It would seem so," Naomi muttered. "I believe he got my number from my uncle's cell phone that's missing. The demented killer apparently wants to taunt me as the next of kin."

"That's scary." Sophia's voice cracked as her brow creased.

"It gets worse… My uncle's house was bugged." Naomi sighed. "Someone's been watching, listening to him…and apparently me, before the devices were discovered by the police."

"Seriously?" Sophia's head snapped back. "That's too creepy."

"Tell me about it," Naomi groaned. "I'm afraid it might have been the work of the unsub." She wondered if this could be only the tip of the iceberg into just how far this person might be willing to go in terrorizing her.

"Please tell me you're not still staying at that house."

"I'm not." She paused thoughtfully. "Actually, I'm staying at Dylan's cabin—"

Sophia's eyes flashed. "You mean Detective Dylan Hester, the same guy you dumped two years ago?"

"Yes, that Dylan," Naomi almost hesitated to say. She didn't exactly consider what she did as dumping Dylan. They had never officially broken off their relationship. It was more of an unspoken reality, given that they lived so far apart, it was impractical to stay together and somehow make it work. "He offered me temporary shelter and, well, I took it, rather than stay at a hotel…and possibly be an open target for a serial killer—"

"You don't have to explain," Sophia said understandingly. "The most important thing is to keep you safe till you can come back home—that is, Miami," she made clear.

"That was what I was thinking," Naomi told her, pushing aside other implications in so doing. While the idea of remaining in Pebble Creek and falling back into Dylan's muscular arms had its appeal, she understood that the career she had worked hard for was elsewhere. She hoped he could respect that.

Sophia seemed to think otherwise. "Of course, that doesn't mean you can't take a trip down memory lane in the bedroom, for old times' sake, if both parties agree."

"I'll keep that in mind." Naomi laughed, finding she needed that at this moment. "Right now, I just want to get through the funeral without crying my eyes out." She jutted her chin. "And not allow my imagination to get carried away in believing that a serial killer is around every bend in the road, waiting to get me."

"Maybe it was your imagination," allowed Sophia, "and maybe not. Just be careful. Serial killers can be pretty calculating, if nothing else. Finding weak spots to keep potential targets on their heels is how they roll in playing a demented game of hiding-in-plain-view-and-seek."

"I know." Naomi twisted her lips, welcoming Sophia's coolheaded and knowledgeable perspective. "I'll be fine. Better let you go."

Sophia nodded. "Keep me informed on anything else that comes up."

"I will." Naomi gave her a smile and signed off. Afterward, she started the car again and drove back onto the street. She cautiously glanced at the rearview mirror, as if expecting the other SUV to reemerge ominously. It did not, thank goodness. She debated whether to burden Dylan with this or not, given that he already had his plate full with the Violet Killer case and the investigation into her uncle's murder, with the two apparently joined at the hip. Shelving the musings, Naomi turned her attention to paying a visit to the funeral home and the eventual burial of her uncle Roger.

Chapter Six

The Violet Killer Task Force gathered for its weekly meeting in a conference room at the Pebble Creek PD—the stakes getting higher by the day for bringing the case to a close with the capture of the unsub, whose adeptness at avoiding identification and apprehension caused tempers to flare. No one wanted to be held responsible for another strangulation death of a victim, with the serial killer seemingly laughing in their collective faces. At least this was how Dylan saw it as he waited his turn to speak while sitting at the rectangular meeting room table.

Standing at the podium was FBI Special Agent Patricia Stabler. The attractive criminal profiler and member of the Bureau's National Center for Analysis of Violent Crime was in her late thirties, tall and slender with crimson hair styled in a long, textured pixie cut that flattered her round face and green eyes. Wearing a sleek tan mélange pantsuit and black leather mules, she was all business when it came to doing her job. Even if it meant at the expense of her marriage, which had reportedly ended largely due to Special Agent Stabler's dedication to the job, believing her personal sacrifice was worthwhile when it meant pursuing dangerous criminals and bringing them to justice. Dylan couldn't decide whether to admire or reject her position. Yes, putting everything you had into your work was indeed admirable. But not if it had a detrimental effect on your love life, which was more important to him at the end of the day.

He wondered if choosing between career and a serious relationship could ever be so simple. Would he really be prepared to walk away from the job for love, as opposed to fighting like hell to preserve both? Dylan thought about Naomi. She, too, had chosen career over a relationship and possible family down the line—never putting herself in the position Patricia Stabler had. Was this by design, so as not to have the hard choices?

Dylan kicked himself for thinking that. Was it selfish of him to have wanted Naomi all to himself, never mind what she wanted? Whatever his regrets where it concerned their previous involvement, he was certain that she was more than capable of balancing a love life and whatever it entailed, including children, with any professional pursuits. He respected her too much to think otherwise. She simply had to want it bad enough someday. He wouldn't fault her for pursuing a dream, any more than he would fault himself for following his own dream of joining the military and police force. If he and Naomi were meant to be, it could still happen. If not, she would forever remain in his heart. Even if he had to fight hard to keep her and these feelings at arm's length.

He turned his attention to Special Agent Stabler as she methodically went through the ins and outs of their unsub in a deep, throaty voice, and the sense of urgency in tracking him down.

"The man we're dealing with here almost certainly suffers from narcissistic personality disorder—or an exaggerated sense of self-importance, while at the same time, possessing a pretty low self-esteem—and can definitely be characterized as having antisocial personality disorder. Not unlike other serial murderers—Ted Bundy, Gary Ridgway, John Wayne Gacy, Gerald Gallego or even Jack the Ripper himself, the consummate unsub serial killer. While he's not the typical sexual predator or child molester murderer such as these, our unsub is every bit as cold and calculating and a true psychopath, if there ever was one." Patricia slid a hand through her hair and pursed thin lips. "He handpicks his victims the same way people study and select the perfect peaches or tomatoes from the grocery store. Whether or not he had a rough childhood, an overbearing mother or some other psychological hang-ups is immaterial, per se, to the fact that he is fully in control of the situation. Or at least he thinks he is. Till we can prove him wrong." She took a deep breath and her eyes blinked. "In his head, the unsub is on a mission in his attacks on the women in this town. He won't quit on his own. He can't, even if he wanted to. That's not how it works with serial homicidal maniacs. The fact that he has chosen to divert from killing only women is only by necessity in his warped and pompous mind. It's not likely to stick. Nevertheless, he's effectively challenging everyone in this room to step up and figure it all out, before he strikes again—or after..."

Dylan took that as his cue and, as the lead detective on the case, went to the podium, alongside Detective Gregory Hwang.

"You ready for this?" Hwang whispered in his ear.

Dylan understood that he was asking due to the delicate nature of a serial killer crime case involving not only his mentor, Roger, but ex-girlfriend, Naomi, who had become part of the investigation, like it or not. "Yeah, I can handle it," he assured Hwang as much as himself. Turning to his fellow Task Force members, with a nod to Patricia Stabler and Police Chief Vernon Frazier, Dylan spoke coolly. "Let's bring everyone up to date on where things stand at the moment."

He walked over to one of the side-by-side large bulletin boards. On it were oversize headshots of seven women and one man. Dylan began with the women. "These are the known victims of the so-called Violet Killer." He stretched out his long arm and, pointing a long finger, named them one by one as if for the first time in respecting their unfortunate and untimely demise. "Conchita Kaplan, twenty-four, a schoolteacher. Linda Allen, thirty-one, a lawyer. Yancy Herrera, twenty-six, a hairstylist. Odette Wolfe, twenty-nine, a waitress. Rosa Vasquez, thirty-three, a dancer. Madison Cherish, thirty, a novelist.

And Vera Bartlett, twenty-two, a senior at Pebble Creek College, became the latest female victim four days ago. In each case, the victim died from ligature strangulation, with the killer's calling card being a single blue violet placed strategically between the lips of each woman as if a work of art. The location of death varied from the victim's own residence to a parking garage to the woods—basically wherever the unsub found most opportune to strike."

Dylan sucked in a deep breath, knowing the newest victim would be the most difficult to talk about. He looked up at the smiling face of the man who had taught him so much about being a police detective, for whom he would never be able to thank enough, and that opportunity had been forever taken away from him. "Two days ago, a former member of our detective team, Roger Lincoln, was found shot to death in his office, where he worked as a private investigator. Roger continued to be connected to the department as a consultant on the Violet Killer case." Dylan paused, closing his eyes and opening them again to gaze at the photograph of the man. "We have reason to believe that Roger was a victim of our serial killer. A violet was left in his mouth by the unsub. Apparently, Roger had managed to crack the case in identifying the perp and was on the verge of blowing this thing wide open when he was killed in a desperate effort to keep him forever silent. But there was a witness.

"Roger was having a video chat on his laptop when he was gunned down." Again, Dylan needed to take a moment as he turned away from the board as Naomi's beautiful face filled his head. He hated that she had to see what she did and live with it for the rest of her life, but this was where things were because of the unsub's actions. "He was speaking to his niece, Naomi Lincoln, a Secret Service agent based in Miami. Some of you may remember that, two years ago, Naomi worked with the department as a crime victims service coordinator for Blane County before moving on. According to her, Roger was on the verge of revealing who the Violet Killer was, before someone crept up behind him and executed him in front of Naomi's very eyes. She never saw or heard the unsub, but he doesn't know that for certain, putting her at risk. Naomi is back in town for Roger's funeral and staying with me." He squared his shoulders, not ducking from where he stood in wanting to protect her. "We have history. Besides that, the perp took Roger's laptop and cell phone, giving him vital information, including Naomi's cell phone number, which he has used to harass her in text messages. If that isn't enough, we've learned that Roger's house and office have been bugged, maybe by the unsub, hoping to gather more damaging info. Or worse, further target Naomi. Until we know for sure one way or the other, or we have someone in custody to that effect, I'll do what I can to keep her safe."

"I wouldn't expect anything less," Police Chief Frazier spoke approvingly. At sixty-two and African American, he was a twenty-five-year veteran of the force, having transferred there from the Portland

Police Bureau as a young detective and worked his way up. "I think everyone in this room has the greatest respect for Roger Lincoln, one of the finest detectives we've had. Making sure nothing happens to his niece, Naomi, is something he would expect from us."

Dylan nodded appreciatively at the baldheaded and brawny chief, who wore tortoiseshell glasses over crusty black eyes and had a graying chevron mustache. He was a stand-up guy who allowed his detectives to do their job with minimal interference, adding meaningful input when necessary. "As yet, we have no DNA, fingerprints or other workable evidence to point to anyone in particular as the Violet Killer. That hasn't stopped him from taunting us seemingly every chance he gets, as if we haven't a clue as to how to stop him. With respect to tracking down the violets themselves, or their source, the flower happens to be one of the most popular in Oregon and is widely grown, in addition to being carried by an abundance of nurseries—making it all but impossible to connect the dots to one individual." Dylan sucked in a deep breath and frowned with growing frustration. "This notwithstanding, there have been—and still are, in some cases—viable suspects…" He turned toward Hwang, who took it from there as he walked toward the other bulletin board, where there were enlarged pictures of several men.

"As of now, we've interviewed a number of persons of interest," Hwang said, scratching through the hair on his chin. He then raised his finger to home in on the first one. "Neil Murray, thirty-four, teaches at

Pebble Creek College. He was seen leaving the scene of one of the murders. Trent Oliver, twenty-six, is an unemployed mechanic who showed a hostility toward women. Blade Canfield, twenty-nine, is a trust fund baby who likes to throw money around like it's going out of style, and had a relationship with one of the women that ended badly. Alfonso Mendoza, forty-two, who's been in and out of prison and has a history of stalking pretty women." Hwang gazed at the final photo. "Last but not least there's Zachary Jamieson, a thirty-five-year-old florist employee with a passion for violets, who was found lurking around an area in which one of the victims was killed.

"Murray and Canfield have rock-solid alibis, while Oliver, Mendoza and Jamieson remain persons of interest," Hwang said, returning to the podium. "So far, we haven't been able to place any of them near the crime scene around the time Lincoln was killed. Doesn't mean one wasn't there and perpetrated the act, in addition to strangling the women. We do, however, have a bead on the type and caliber of weapon used to kill Roger Lincoln. A .45 ACP handgun. If we find the murder weapon, everything else may fall into place in taking down the Violet Killer."

Dylan added a few more thoughts, as did Special Agent Stabler and Chief Frazier, before other members of the Task Force weighed in on where they were in the investigation, with everyone on the same page in their determination to achieve the goal of bringing this case to a close with the arrest of the perp before anyone else had to die.

As the meeting broke up, Patricia Stabler caught up to Dylan in the hall. "Hope everything works out for you and Roger Lincoln's niece in terms of having her back while she's in town and in harm's way."

"Thanks." Dylan's eyes flashed at the FBI profiler and wondered if she was alluding to anything beyond his being Naomi's protector, which was probably the most he could hope for at this stage of their lives. "I'll always have her back," he said firmly.

"The FBI often works very closely with the Secret Service, so I applaud her in pursuing that path," Patricia said.

"Naomi loves what she does for a living," he almost hated to admit, but did so anyhow.

"Good for her." Patricia showed her teeth and Dylan wondered if this was one of those career-before-love-life moments. Or was he misreading her?

"The sooner she can get back to it, the better for everyone." Dylan hoped he wasn't giving away his mixed feelings in losing Naomi again to her career. He would do nothing to interfere with it. Especially given the stakes a serial killer had raised in a game of life and death.

"The FBI will continue to use all its tools, Hester, to help bring down the Violet Killer," the profiler contended. "It's one of those make-or-break cases that beg to be cracked and dissected."

Dylan grinned. "Spoken like a true NCAVC professional."

"Just telling it as I see it," she insisted.

"Well, we'll gladly accept all the help we can get from the FBI," he told her, not willing to kick a gift horse in the mouth. Even if it meant jockeying for position in the investigation and sometimes competing strategies for being most effective in solving the case.

Chief Frazier came up to them and stood eye to eye with Dylan, while giving him a vague expression. "Got a sec…?"

"Sure." Dylan watched as Frazier and Patricia shared a few words, before he followed the chief to his office.

It was in a corner on the main floor of the building and spacious with a picture window. The wood blinds were open a crack. On a U-shaped executive desk was a framed photograph of Vernon Frazier and his wife of forty years, Evelyn. It reminded Dylan of what he could still have in a long and lasting romance and marriage, should this opportunity present itself with the right woman. Naomi immediately came to mind, whether he tried to block this thought or not.

"Have a seat," Frazier voiced tonelessly.

Dylan sat in one of two office chairs while watching his boss plop down onto his own massage desk chair, wondering what this was all about. He guessed it pertained to the investigation.

"How's Naomi doing?" Frazier peered at him through coal eyes.

"She's coping," Dylan answered as best he could. "Like us, she wants answers as to why this had to happen to her uncle as well as the other victims of the Violet Killer."

"Yeah, I understand. Roger and I go back a long way. I never wanted him to retire, but... Well, you know the man. His pride wouldn't allow him to take a step back." Deep furrows lined Frazier's forehead. "Maybe if he had stayed on the force, it might have been a different outcome."

Dylan agreed, but as nature had already taken its course, said, "We'll never know."

"What has Naomi, whom I've heard good things about as a member of the Secret Service, told you about what she witnessed on the laptop?"

"Only what I already mentioned. She saw Roger get shot, but not who shot him."

"Maybe she remembers more than she thinks," Frazier suggested, leaning forward.

Dylan sat back. "Not sure I follow you."

"In times of great stress, people often block out the hardest things to remember. That may or may not be the case here, but as she's staying with you, it doesn't hurt to press Naomi for any useful information you can derive from her that might be pertinent to solving this case."

"I'll see what I can do." Even then, Dylan was concerned that pressing her too hard might be counterproductive. And even resentful on Naomi's part. But at the same time, if she could fill in a blank or two, wouldn't she want to do that, if it meant identifying a serial killer on the loose?

Frazier shifted his body. "Good. At this point, we

can use all the help we can get." His cell phone rang and he answered. Dylan watched the chief's face darken before he hung up.

"What is it?" Dylan asked.

"A young woman has been reported missing," Frazier spoke, sounding ill at ease. "She could be yet another victim of the Violet Killer."

DYLAN WAS GLUM when he passed the unsettling news on to Naomi later that afternoon by the lake, where he found her standing on the grass outside his house. "Her name is Sandra Neville. The twenty-nine-year-old orthodontist was supposed to meet her parents for dinner last night. When she didn't show up or call, both uncharacteristic according to them, they naturally became worried, given the current state of affairs, and filed a missing person report."

Naomi cringed. "Do you think she's dead...?"

Without saying it, Dylan knew she was asking specifically if the orthodontist may have fallen into the clutches of the Violet Killer. Though he feared this might well be true, he didn't want to immediately jump to the worst-case scenario. "Hopefully, she simply lost track of time," he threw out unevenly.

"But what if she didn't?" Naomi questioned. "What if he has her...and she's still alive and needs to be rescued before it's too late...?"

"We're doing everything we can to try to find Ms. Neville," he sought to assure her. "The fact that she was reported missing in less than twenty-four hours gives us more time to work with." His voice dropped an octave when carrying on. "Unfortunately, if she has encountered the Violet Killer unsub, it could be too late to save her. From what we know, the perp has typically stalked his victims and when ready to attack, has done so in rather quick fashion. But again, we're not there yet, so let's just take a wait-and-see approach."

Naomi tucked a loose hair behind her ear and he sensed she had something on her mind. She looked up at him and said with a catch to her voice, "This may or may not be anything, but something happened earlier today…"

"What?" Dylan tensed.

"Well, I could've sworn that someone tried to run me off the road." She waited a beat. "Or at least intended to frighten me half to death."

Dylan didn't like the sound of that, all things considered. He glanced around them warily, feeling pretty secure in his surroundings. But even with that, the idea of Naomi being a target to a killer shook him. "Let's go back inside and you can tell me more about this—"

Minutes later, they were seated on the modern chenille sofa, where Naomi wrung her hands. "The car just seemed to come out of nowhere and was on my tail," she contended nervously. "When I put some distance between us, it followed. Finally, it turned onto a side street and that was that. Not sure what to make of it."

"What type of car was it?" Dylan asked.

"It was a dark SUV," she told him. "Not sure what model."

"Could you make out anything on the driver?"

"No, the glass was tinted." Naomi batted her lashes. "Maybe I freaked out for no reason."

"Or maybe for all the right reasons." Dylan jutted his chin. He hated to think that the unsub was privy to Naomi's whereabouts at any given moment. Especially now that she was essentially under his protection and, Dylan wanted to believe, safe from harm.

She frowned. "So, you think that could've been the Violet Killer sending me an unnerving message?"

"Too soon to say," he spoke honestly. "Has he sent you any other text messages?"

"No." She sighed. "That's a relief."

Dylan agreed, believing that if it had been the unsub, he likely would have found it hard to resist taunting her as part of his psychological games. Still, nothing said that the perp couldn't still be toying with them both, keeping him and Naomi guessing as to what he might try next. "I'll check if the vehicle you described matches any owned by our current list of suspects," Dylan said. "In the meantime, if anything like that happens again, let me know pronto."

"I will," she promised and gave him a deadpan look. "Hopefully, the missing woman will show up soon and everyone can breathe a little easier."

He seconded that, but his instincts told Dylan that this might not end well for Sandra Neville, even if the cause for her disappearance was something—or someone—other than the Violet Killer.

Chapter Seven

Saturday was overcast, matching the somber mood of Naomi as she stood beside Dylan at the Pebble Creek Cemetery for the funeral of her uncle, Roger Lincoln. She was wearing a dark gray dress suit and low-heeled black pumps, and she'd put her hair in an updo style for the sad occasion. As difficult as it had been when attending her parents' funeral two decades ago, this may have been even more painful, if that was possible. Aside from being old enough to truly appreciate the loss, Naomi couldn't imagine anything worse than losing a loved one to violence and witnessing it all at once. Her only solace was that her uncle Roger had found his way to a place alongside his brother, Milton Lincoln, where they and Naomi's mother, Paula, could be at peace.

Eyeing Dylan in a black suit that fit well on his frame and made him look even more handsome than usual, Naomi felt grateful for his support and friendship through this trying time. She knew it was just as difficult for him, mourning the loss and trying to find Roger's killer. Last night, she'd been sure another nightmare of the shooting would happen. Especially after Dylan had told her about a missing woman who was possibly another victim of the madman on the prowl. But to Naomi's surprise, she had slept without any bad dreams she could remember. Perhaps it was due to feeling Dylan's powerful presence, even if in another room; knowing he was just a shout away should the bogeyman come after her in nightmares or reality. And what about when it was time to return to her real world? Would the specter of her uncle's tragic death continue to haunt her like a woman possessed?

Naomi gazed at the mourners, recognizing some and not others. She couldn't help but wonder if her uncle's murderer had actually dared to show his face while hiding in plain view, for some kind of sick gratification. She'd heard that this was the maniacal manner in which some killers got their kicks right under the noses of law enforcement—which, in this case, was on guard and sprinkled throughout the cemetery should trouble arise—even while the unsub gave the guise of being present for the right reasons. She sensed by his intense demeanor and shifting eyes that Dylan was thinking the same thing. Had they always been on the same wavelength when it counted most? Or was she mixing apples and oranges when sizing him up and regretting the way things ended between them two years ago?

Naomi turned her attention to Pastor Krista Gilliam as the attractive and slender thirtysomething woman picked up on where she left off in the church, focusing on Roger's career and love of the community. Caught up in the emotion, Naomi wept and found herself holding on to Dylan for support. He seemed comfortable with it and placed a long arm around her waist.

"You okay?" he whispered sympathetically.

"I will be," she promised him, knowing it was what her uncle would have wanted, in spite of his untimely demise.

After the gravesite eulogies, Naomi greeted mourners, thanking them for coming. Police Chief Vernon Frazier took her hand in his while offering his condolences. "I'm so sorry about this, Naomi," he voiced from the heart. "Roger was a fine man who always spoke very highly of you."

Naomi's eyes crinkled. "I felt the same way about him."

"If you need anything, let me know," the chief said.

"I will."

Detective Gregory Hwang expressed his sympathies, followed by other members of the Pebble Creek PD. Naomi was then approached by a tall, slim redhaired woman in a dark gray striped two-piece skirt suit and matching heels. "FBI Special Agent Patricia Stabler," she identified herself. "I never got to meet your uncle, but from what I've heard, he was a highly regarded member of the police force." She reached into the pocket of her suit jacket and pulled out a card. "If you ever need to talk about what happened, I'm a criminal profiler and investigative psychologist, ready to help."

Naomi took the card and nodded. "Thank you." She watched as Agent Stabler moved on to Dylan and the two exchanged a few words. Obviously, they were working together on the case. Still, Naomi couldn't help but wonder if the pretty FBI profiler was his type. Or if he was in any way interested in her. Naomi quickly dismissed the thought from her head, realizing that she had no claim on Dylan to feel jealousy. To suggest otherwise would be to give in to feelings that both had apparently put behind them, to one degree or another. No matter how difficult it was to bear.

The last person to pay respects was a petite, well-dressed African American woman in her early fifties with brunette hair in a buzz cut. "Hi," she said nervously, taking Naomi's hand and squeezing it. "My name's Brenda Quinlan. I was dating your uncle when he passed."

"Really?" Naomi raised a brow at her, taken aback by the news. Not that her uncle Roger had talked much about his love life, as he was a very private man when it came to his own romance. Having never married, he seemed fairly content to spend his life alone for the most part. When had that changed?

"We'd only been out on a few dates," she explained as if reading Naomi's mind. "He was a good man and talked about you all the time. I'm so sorry for your loss."

"Yours, as well," Naomi had to say graciously.

She wished they had gotten to know one another when Uncle Roger was still alive. He deserved to have someone special in his life. Naomi felt the same way about herself. But was it too late for that? She turned to Dylan, who was now speaking to Brenda, as if they were old friends. Naomi wondered if he was as lonely as she felt at times. Or had they each made their own beds to lie in by themselves?

"DID YOU KNOW Uncle Roger was seeing someone?" Naomi asked from the passenger seat of Dylan's official vehicle.

"He never mentioned that to me," Dylan responded levelly as he drove them to the lawyer's office, where Roger's will would be divulged. It had surprised him that Roger had included him in the will. As far as Dylan was concerned, he didn't want anything that Naomi should have. "I'm sure if things had gotten serious, Roger would've let both of us in on it."

"I suppose." Her voice cracked. "Brenda seems like a nice person."

"I agree." Dylan felt that Naomi was nice, too. But that wasn't enough to seal the deal in giving them the type of relationship he had dreamed of. Maybe things wouldn't have worked out for Roger, either, once they got past the get-along-with-each-other stage. No one would ever know for sure now. He couldn't help but think that the same was true with him and Naomi. They were both alive and well, but still not on the same page in their pursuits in life, which no longer included each other.

"Do you think the unsub was at the cemetery?" Naomi broke into Dylan's musings.

"It's possible, but probably not," he responded confidently. To Dylan, the funeral was somber enough without the person responsible for Roger's death rearing his ugly head. That didn't mean the perp wasn't brazen enough to try to show his face. But with the grounds blanketed by cops and the FBI, it didn't seem to be in the cards for the Violet Killer to press his luck by overplaying his hand. "My guess is the unsub is lying low for the time being, waiting for the right time and place to make his next move."

"Maybe he's already made it," Naomi spoke glumly and Dylan read between the lines. "Any more news on the missing woman?"

"She's still unaccounted for," Dylan hated to say, staring through the windshield as he approached a red light. Sandra Neville had been missing for more than thirty-six hours, a troubling sign if ever there was one. But he, for one, wasn't about to give up hope that she might still be alive. "Search and rescue teams are out in force throughout the county, trying to find her. We won't give up till we know her whereabouts and condition, one way or the other."

"I can't imagine what her family must be going through at the moment." Naomi took a breath. "Then again, I guess I have some idea. I just buried my uncle, and no amount of hoping will ever bring him back."

"True." Dylan could hardly counter that reality. He could try, though, to look at it another way. "However,

Roger left behind something precious that he would want to stay strong in his absence, and that's you."

"I know," she said emotionally and faced him. "Uncle Roger would want that for both of us."

Dylan glanced at her with a smooth grin. "So why don't we try our best to adhere to his wishes, even under the cloud of his killer still at large."

Naomi's shoulders squared acceptingly. "Okay, I'm with you and Uncle Roger. I'll try to abide by his wishes."

"Deal," Dylan seconded, and wondered if he, too, was up to the task, with the unsub continuing to cause headaches and a woman still missing to be concerned about.

NAOMI AND DYLAN entered the law office of Benjamin Gardner, Roger's attorney. The seventysomething, white-haired man was tall and on the frail side, wearing a skinny-fit dark blue suit. They shook his hand and sat on brown tweed visitor chairs, while Benjamin took a seat on a midback black leather chair behind a sprawling vintage wood desk.

"Thanks for coming," he said, adjusting silver wire-rimmed glasses. "My condolences for your loss. Roger was a good friend and will be missed in that regard and as a client of longstanding." He paused and fiddled with some papers on his desk, as if to find something to do with his hands. "Anyway, let's get down to business."

Naomi was admittedly a bit nervous as she waited to see what her uncle had decided upon in what turned out to be his final act, without his being the wiser. She wasn't really surprised to see that he had left Dylan something in his will. After all, the two remained close even after her uncle quit the force. Whatever the case, she was totally fine with it, wanting only to settle his estate and see where she went from there. She glanced at Dylan and he glanced back with a comforting grin before gazing at the lawyer with what she believed was largely curiosity.

When he spoke again, Benjamin said simply, in giving Naomi a direct look, "Roger left his property, including the house and land, to you, Ms. Lincoln, along with his car, savings, stocks and bonds, and proceeds from his life insurance and place of business, once liquidated." He took a breath as Naomi considered her uncle's generosity and the attorney turned Dylan's way. "As for you, Mr. Hester, Roger left money for you to buy that powerboat you've always dreamed of, wanting to make sure you had no more excuses for putting it off." Dylan looked clearly taken aback and humbled as he gave a chuckle. "He also bequeathed to you a photograph Roger took of you and Ms. Lincoln, which he considered his favorite. I believe it is sitting on the mantel in the living room of your house, Naomi."

She smiled thoughtfully. "I'll make sure he gets it," she said, regarding Dylan and remembering the occasion when the photo was taken.

"Oh, and uh, Roger also wanted me to pass along that you should keep an eye on his niece," the attorney told Dylan, "no matter where she hangs her hat."

Dylan seemed to contemplate the somewhat un-usual wish, before breaking into a half grin and peering at Naomi. "I can do that," he promised in a determined voice, causing her heart to skip a beat in the moment. Was this her uncle speaking from the grave in doing his part to see to it that they stayed connected, even if apart?

"Well, that's it," Benjamin said, as if glad to be done. "Any questions?"

Twenty minutes later, Naomi and Dylan sat at a booth in Lesley's Restaurant for lunch. It was a popu-lar hangout for law enforcement, specializing in sea-food and desserts. It also happened to be where they had their first official date, bringing back memories, mostly pleasant, for Naomi. She wondered if Dylan was feeling it, too. Asking, though, was not an op-tion, in case he had gotten too far past that time in their lives to want to go back, even in thought.

"If I'm not mistaken," Dylan said, as if reading her mind while studying the menu, "on our first date here, you ordered the crispy shrimp and buttered noodles. Correct me if I'm wrong…"

Naomi couldn't help but blush and be impressed at the same time. "You're not wrong," she admitted. "You're spot-on."

He flashed his teeth smugly. "Shall we try it again?" he challenged her.

She accepted. "Sure, why not."

Dylan ordered the same lunch and both also or-dered lemonade to down it. "Just like old times, huh?"

Naomi wasn't sure she was prepared to go quite that far, but liked the notion anyhow. She forked a shrimp. "I suppose it is."

"I guess Roger wanted to do his part to make sure we didn't forget the good times," Dylan said, his voice lingering.

"I think you're right." She went for the noodles. "So, when do you plan to buy the boat?" Naomi imagined being on it with him for a day on the lake.

"As soon as I get this business with the unsub behind me." Dylan ate shrimp and Naomi found she enjoyed watching him eat. "How about you? What are your plans for the house you now own?"

Her eyes flashed. "Haven't really thought about it," she confessed. Not with everything else that had gone on. "I'll probably put it on the market." Would it make any sense to hold on to the property if she lived elsewhere? Wouldn't keeping the house only bring up sad memories?

"Maybe a good idea," Dylan said flatly. "I'm sure you could fetch a pretty good price in a hot market these days—even more with a first-rate security system installed ahead of time for the next owner."

Naomi dabbed a napkin to her mouth. She agreed she should have it installed, whether living there or not, if only to add to the property's value. "You're right," she said, then listened as he suggested a home security company to get in touch with.

"So, I suppose you'll be heading back to Miami now that the funeral is over...?"

Her lashes fluttered. "Are you trying to get rid

of me?" Maybe she had overstayed her welcome at his cabin.

"Believe me, that's the last thing on my mind." His earnest look was convincing.

"Then what?"

He sat back and sighed. "I just thought that as long as the Violet Killer unsub was seemingly targeting you, it might be a good thing if you left town, if only for the time being. Of course, if you wanted to come back after he's been brought down, you'd be more than welcome to do so."

Naomi waited a long beat, trying to gauge his words. Was he inviting her to return after the dust settled, to maybe try to pick up where they left off two years ago? Or was she overthinking, as usual? Did they really have a chance to make things work when her life was now elsewhere? As it was, she had been giving the timing of her departure some thought. She wondered if he would agree with her plans, while looking him in the eye. "Actually, I think I'd like to stay here for a while longer."

"Really?" Dylan cocked a brow in surprise while holding his glass of lemonade.

"Yes. With Uncle Roger's killer still on the loose, I feel as if I need to do something to help."

"Such as…?" He peered at her uncomfortably.

"I don't know," she said, moving food around her plate. "Maybe join in on the search for Sandra Neville."

Dylan frowned. "Are you sure that's a good idea?"

"Why not?" Naomi remained resolute in her decision. "She's missing and her family is worried sick from what I've heard, and understandably so. Every second that goes by where she's not found is like sticking a dagger into the hearts of those praying that Sandra's still alive. I wouldn't want anyone to have to deal with what I've just gone through, if there's any way possible to prevent it. If I can help to locate her, one way or the other, I want to do that."

He continued to eye her skeptically. "Don't you have an assignment to get back to?"

"My boss has given me some space to deal with Uncle Roger's death," she reported. "I'm sure he would be okay with a few more days to that effect." Nevertheless, Naomi intended to convey this to him, to be sure it met with his approval.

"We could always use extra volunteers in the search," Dylan conceded, shifting to one side. "You have my support, but only if you continue staying at my house for as long as you're in Pebble Creek. It's still safer there for you while the Violet Killer is ter-rorizing women—and possibly targeting you—and would allow me to keep an eye on you more success-fully, in honoring Roger's wishes."

Naomi couldn't help but smile, feeling comforted at the idea of him being her handsome protector, even if she was more than capable of protecting herself from a serial killer. One could never be capable enough, she knew. "You drive a hard bargain, Detective."

The lines around Dylan's mouth remained inflex-ible. "So, is it a deal?" he pressed.

She laughed. "Yes, it's a deal."

"Good." He finally softened his protective stance

and gulped down the rest of his lemonade. "Why don't we swing by your new house and pick up the photograph Roger so generously passed on to me."

"Great idea," she said, while conjuring up poignant memories that would probably be best if remained buried in the photo.

AFTER CHECKING THE house for any signs of an intruder, they ended up in front of the fireplace mantel, where Dylan lifted the photograph that Roger had left him in his will. Studying it, Dylan was struck at just how handsome they looked as a couple. Naomi, dressed in a wine-red printed sports bra and white denim shorts, was every bit as shapely and sexy as she was today.

"Nice, huh?" he remarked openly, holding it at an angle so they could share the visual.

"Yes," she said, smiling. "We had fun that day."

"Yeah." Dylan gazed at the picture again. What he wouldn't give to go back in time and relive being a couple at the county fair and well on their way to being in love. How could he have known that a year later, they would unexpectedly go their separate ways and his heart would end up broken? But life always threw you curves. It was how one responded to this that defined the person. Training his eyes upon Naomi's gorgeous face, Dylan drifted his gaze down to her generous mouth. It was open just a tad and seemed inviting him to kiss. The overwhelming urge to capitulate was more than he was able or willing to pass up. Lifting her chin, he kissed those lips and braced himself for a flat-out rejection of the advance. Instead, she allowed the kiss to linger, seemingly as into it as he was. Though the surge of desire rolled through him like a tsunami, he forced himself to pull back.

Naomi, batting her eyes, touched her mouth. "What was that all about?"

Dylan asked himself the same question. He wanted it to be about possibilities for the future with a pinch hit from the past. But he knew better than to get his hopes up for something that was likely out of reach. Grinning crookedly, he responded, "Just a kiss for old times' sake. Sorry if I overstepped."

"It's fine," she said tonelessly. "Maybe we both needed that for closure."

He frowned, not liking the sound of that, but not surprised, considering where they were at this stage of their lives. Which was definitely not together. The sooner he reconciled with that, the better he could be happy for her living in Miami as a Secret Service agent. With possibly some other guy waiting in the wings.

"Whatever you say," Dylan voiced thickly. "Let's get out of here."

She nodded stiffly, seemingly content to leave it at that.

Chapter Eight

Later that afternoon, Naomi threw on cuffed boy-friend jeans and a knit top to go with her slip-on sneakers and put her hair into a ponytail while wearing a black running cap, before joining other volunteers in the search for Sandra Neville. They were in a wooded area not far from her house that had already apparently been searched to no avail. But the belief among authorities was that, in many instances, it was the second or third try that yielded results, for better or worse. Naomi hoped it was for the better in finding the missing woman alive. She was in a group of four people—two women and two men—between the ages of early twenties and midseventies. They were all on a first-name basis and everyone seemed friendly enough and fully vested in the mission set forth. Though Naomi felt at ease with them, it occurred to her that some kidnappers and killers got a perverse thrill in blending in with searchers, while putting on a perfectly innocent front. Could whoever was responsible for Sandra's disappearance be hiding in clear view?

Breaking away from that unsettling thought, Naomi went back to the unexpected kiss earlier that reverberated throughout her bones. Still reeling from it, she had almost forgotten the impact Dylan's potent kisses had on her mind and body. It came back loud and clear like a romance movie in living color. He was the lover who took her up into the clouds, higher and higher, wanting more. But circumstances had brought her back down to earth. No matter how much she still felt for him, Naomi doubted the same was true in reverse. Asking Dylan for a second chance at a long-distance relationship was likely a path he wasn't interested in. Could she really blame him? Was it not a recipe for disaster?

Her focus again shifted as she found herself slightly ahead of the others, having gone farther than the perimeter established by the law enforcement coordinating the search. Naomi was just about to turn around after plowing through some dense shrubbery beneath the trees, when her eyes landed on a frail and dirty human arm sticking out like a sore thumb from the undergrowth. Naomi's heart skipped a beat. Even without seeing the rest of the body, she sensed that the search for Sandra Neville had come to a tragic end.

DYLAN ARRIVED AT the scene with a heavy heart. He knew it was a long shot—and longer with each passing hour that she remained missing—that Sandra Neville would be found alive. Now it appeared as if the worst-case scenario had occurred. At least this was what had been conveyed to him, as he approached the crime scene tape. Along with the fact that it was Naomi who first discovered the corpse. Spotting her now, being comforted by other search volunteers, outside the perimeters of where the investigation was underway, Dylan had to put aside an urge to go over and take her into his arms. That would come later. And any second thoughts on her insistence upon staying in town and being part of the investigation unofficially and indirectly into the killing of Roger. Right now, it was important, for both their sakes, that he put first his role as the lead investigator of the Violet Killer case.

Climbing over the yellow tape with his long legs, Dylan met up with Detective Hwang and Agent Patricia Stabler, who were standing just feet from the deceased woman.

"Is it her?" Dylan asked to confirm, shifting his gaze from one to the other.

"Yeah, afraid so," Hwang uttered bleakly.

"Her ID makes that clear," Patricia added, holding it up in front of him with a nitrile-gloved hand. "It was on her person. Sandra Adrienne Neville, age twenty-nine."

Dylan frowned and gazed down at the fully clothed decedent. Even with the sun's rays starting to weaken, filtering down through the trees at this time of day, and her body partly obscured by the scrubs, he could see that she was slender and African American, with black hair styled in a side-swept undercut. She almost appeared to be sleeping, with her head lying slanted on a pillow of underbrush.

"Any signs of foul play?" he asked.

"There's bruising on her neck and wrists," Patricia pointed out. "She definitely put up a struggle with someone…"

"Looks like that someone is our unsub," Hwang said. "A cursory gloved check in her mouth indicated that stuck inside is a blue violet, courtesy of the Violet Killer. We left it there for forensics and the medical examiner to duke it out over."

Dylan's brow furrowed. This was the first African American victim of the unsub, illustrating his willingness to go after any women who fit the general description of those he targeted as young, attractive and available to put down. More concerning to Dylan was how this was affecting Naomi. Already considered a potential target of the serial killer and biracial, did this freak her out? Put her in any greater danger?

Hwang, seemingly reading into that, wrinkled his nose. "If Naomi hadn't spotted the decedent outside the boundaries, we might never have found her—"

"I know," Dylan conceded musingly. "Still, after witnessing Roger's murder and now this—I just wonder how much more she can take…" It was a question he wasn't sure he wanted to know the answer to.

"Maybe more than you think." Patricia gave him a knowing look. "If they thought she couldn't cut it, the Secret Service would never have brought her on board, trust me." She put a hand on his arm. "Go talk to her." Patricia sighed, removing her hand. "Anything might help—"

"I will." He nodded in agreement, while acknowledging in his head that Naomi was more than capable of dealing with adversity, even if his natural instincts were to want to shield her from uncomfortable circumstances. Right now, his best bet was to be there to support her for at least as long as she was in town. How long that would be was anyone's guess. After her latest traumatic episode, maybe now she would decide it was best to head back to Miami, as far away from the perp and his homicidal urges as possible. If that happened, they would go from there on the nature of their continuing involvement.

Before Dylan could make his way to Naomi, the medical examiner arrived. Dr. Martha Donahue was in her early forties and small with short caramel balayage hair in feathery curls. She touched her white-framed glasses as she approached the three. "Came as soon as I could," she said, sounding exhausted as though having just run a marathon. "What are we looking at?"

"A deceased African American female," Dylan said reluctantly. "Appears as though she's the victim of foul play in a manner consistent with other young women who have recently fallen prey to a serial killer."

"Looks like she put up a fight," Patricia said, "and, hopefully, took some DNA from her attacker."

"We'll see." Martha narrowed her small blue eyes and slid on a pair of white cotton gloves, before crouching and beginning a visual and physical inspection of the victim. Dylan never felt particularly comfortable with this aspect of criminal investigations, where decedents were no longer able to call the shots in terms of privacy and dignity. He wished Sandra could open her mouth and tell them as much as she could in helping to find her killer. Forensic examination and an autopsy would have to suffice. He watched the medical examiner delicately manipulating the victim's neck. "Judging by the condition of the neck area, my preliminary assessment is that the decedent died from strangulation caused by some kind of ligature." She turned her attention to one of the victim's hands. "Looks like there may be some blood under the fingernails, indicating the killer may have left behind some DNA, if not her own."

"How long has she been dead, Doc?" Hwang asked.

Martha examined more of the corpse. "If I had to make a preliminary guess, I'd say it's been less than forty-eight hours."

Dylan winced. This would indicate that Sandra Neville was likely murdered close to the time she went missing and at the location where the body was found. He suspected that she may have gone for a short hike, where she ran into her killer, who in accordance with his pattern of behavior, lay in wait, catching her off guard. At that point, she was pretty much the perp's for the taking.

He watched as the medical examiner removed the unsub's calling card from the victim's mouth, holding

up the wet and discolored violet, as if it was a tro-
phy. "Looks as though your Violet Killer has struck
again," Martha stated grimly.

"Yeah, I was afraid of that," Dylan muttered with
resignation. With another person added to the unsub's list of victims, Dylan could think only that he
would be damned if Naomi were to be next. He made
his way over to her as she was still huddled around
the group of volunteers who shared the grisly discov-
ery with Naomi. She reacted when seeing him and he
wasn't quite sure what she may have been thinking.
He pulled her away to a spot where they could speak
alone. "Hey," he said evenly. "How are you doing?"

"Not too good." Naomi pursed her lips. "This is
quickly becoming a nightmare."

Those sentiments were perfectly understandable
to Dylan. How could they not be? He had come to
the same conclusion—only drawn out over the last
two years plus. But gazing at her face and lowered
eyes, he sensed that there was something more going
on. "What is it?"

She gazed up at him and pulled her cell phone
out of a pocket. "I just received this text message…"

Dylan looked at the small screen and read:

She reminded me of you. Still, a poor substitute for
the real Naomi Lincoln. See you soon…

Alarmed that the unsub had again threatened
Naomi and was possibly watching them at that moment, Dylan guided her back to the other volunteers.

He sized each one up in assessing their innocence. After some questions and feeling reasonably certain that none were behind the ominous text message, he told Naomi fixedly, "Wait here till I get back. And under no circumstances do you go into the woods on your own."

She batted her lashes. "Don't worry, I'm not going to make myself easy prey for this killer," she insisted. "If it's his intent to come after me, it won't be on his own terms."

Dylan nodded, feeling that she got it. Since she was a federal law enforcement officer herself, he wouldn't have expected anything less. Still, he hated to have to leave her for others to protect. But with the unsub once again snubbing his nose at the entire Task Force for his own sick gratification, catching him had to be a top priority. Especially with another victim already in the books.

THAT NIGHT, NAOMI lay in bed, tossing and turning, while trying hard not to feel guilty about the death of Sandra Neville. Though, rationally speaking, she knew it wasn't her fault that a psycho serial slayer targeted the orthodontist. But in an irrational way, she couldn't help herself. After all, didn't the unsub practically confess that he chose Sandra because she reminded him of her?

Still, a poor substitute for the real Naomi Lincoln. See you soon...

The mere thought gave Naomi a chill. He was telling her she was to be his next victim. Apparently, the

Violet Killer was not only stalking her, but had managed to blend in with the volunteers in the search for Sandra Neville. No doubt, he was laughing his head off at being so close to capture, yet so far. Dylan, FBI Agent Stabler and other law enforcement had immediately fanned out in trying to locate the perp. Alas, with no success. He had apparently come and gone like a thief in the night. Leaving everyone more than a little unnerved and frustrated.

But Naomi refused to allow him to take away her courage as a Secret Service agent and as a woman who knew an intimidator when she saw one. The Violet Killer was not going to send her packing while leaving behind the tortured memory of her uncle, who was ever so close to identifying and helping to put away the unsub, before he himself was taken out instead. She owed Uncle Roger that much to hang around and do what she could to see justice done, even if uncertain how best to achieve that goal while limited in her official capacity. Something told her that Dylan would prefer that she stay out of it, as though her presence would somehow hinder the investigation. Or was it more his need to be her protector in keeping her out of harm's way at all costs?

Either way, Naomi had to be there and could only hope that Dylan could respect that. She was giving him no choice, with them both wanting the same thing at the end of the day. To stop the Violet Killer from terrorizing the community. That notwithstanding, the thought of Dylan holding her in his arms, making love to her, somehow comforted her, even

if he and she were no longer together. She still felt
the pleasant sting of his kiss from earlier in the day.
Was it truly a mere one-off to nostalgia and nothing more? Or a strong indicator that something was
still there between them that needed to be explored?

Shutting her eyes, Naomi drifted off to sleep, fully
expecting another nightmare to surface involving
perhaps the murders of Uncle Roger and Sandra Neville in a frightful convergence. Instead, she got hot
and passionate lovemaking with Dylan that seemed
so real that she became lost in it to the exclusion of
anything else.

IN THE MORNING, Dylan made breakfast while waiting
for Naomi to get up. He'd listened in at her door before calling it a night himself and thought he heard
some soft sounds he couldn't decipher. Resisting the
urge to go in and see if she would welcome his company, he instead retreated to his own room. It would
be foolish to complicate their lives any more than
they already were. With a multiple-murder investigation well underway and Naomi being in the perp's
crosshairs, the last thing either of them needed was
to go down memory lane, clouding their judgment
in the present. Whether she headed back to Miami
now or later, it would happen soon enough. Allowing one kiss to give him hope that they could turn
back the hands of time would not be a smart move
on his part. Been there, done that. No thank you.
He shouldn't go there, if he knew what was best for

him. Or was he prepared to truly say what was best for him and what was not?

His thoughts turned to Sandra Neville, the latest female victim of the Violet Killer. Number eight and counting. But this one came with even more unsettling connotations. She had apparently been targeted with Naomi in mind, if the unsub was to be believed. He had directly threatened her life. This was raising the stakes dangerously and far too close to home for Dylan. Not only was Naomi his one true love who got away, but now she was back and staying with him, if only for a while longer. He was not about to allow a serial killer to take this little time they had together away from them.

Before he could chew more on that thought and get back to work on the griddle, Dylan looked up and saw Naomi walk into the kitchen. She was still in her sleepwear of a purplish chemise and black pajamas shorts, with her hair down and uncombed, and barefoot—all of which turned him on more than he wanted.

"Good morning," she said, rubbing her eyes.

"Good morning." He took a chill pill, trying not to think of just how sexy and inviting she looked at the moment. "Sleep well?"

Naomi blushed thoughtfully. "It was a bit restless, as you might imagine."

"Yeah." How could he not relate? What she had been put through yesterday from sunup to sundown would have made sleep hard to come by for anyone. Or might her erratic sleep pattern have been caused by something more of a carnal nature, like his own restless sleep? "Hungry?"

She nodded. "My stomach is growling." She ran her hand over her flat stomach as if to stifle it.

He wasn't surprised. After picking up a pizza when they got home last night, neither of them ate very much before she went to bed. He, in turn, stayed up longer, making some calls and trying to keep up with the many layers in the Violet Killer investigation. Progress was painfully slow. Yet with each passing day and another victim, they were still putting together clues that would ultimately take down the unsub, one way or the other.

"Good." Dylan grinned at her. "Hope you like blueberry pancakes and bacon." He seemed to recall this was one of her favorite breakfasts once upon a time.

"Yes." Naomi flashed her teeth and seemed to applaud him for remembering. In truth, there wasn't much that he didn't remember when it came to their time together. But he didn't need to tell her that.

"Have a seat and breakfast will be served shortly."

"Thanks." She sat on a stool and tasted the orange juice he had already poured into two glasses. "Anything new on the investigation since last night?"

"Not really," Dylan reported. "The perp got away, but we're still interviewing people and checking out any surveillance cameras leading into and out of the woods."

"Do you think that he actually killed Sandra Neville to get to me?" Naomi's eyes were wide with incredulity.

"I think he'd like for you—frankly, all of us on the Task Force—to believe that to mess with our heads." Dylan set the plate of steaming pancakes and bacon before her on the island. "More likely," he suggested as a good possibility, "Ms. Neville may have been a target for the unsub before you even returned to town and he was simply waiting for the right opportunity to strike. The fact that she happened to be African American was perfect for his mind games. And to keep up with his preying upon women of any color, so as to terrorize all women in Pebble Creek." This sounded plausible to Dylan, even if his gut instincts felt that picking on Naomi as Roger's niece had played some role in the latest victim's death.

"Well, it's definitely working," she commented and bit into a piece of bacon. "What woman in town wouldn't be shaken to the core with what's been happening with seemingly no end in sight?"

"The end will come," Dylan tried to assure her as he set his plate down and plopped onto the stool beside her. "Whether it's Harold Shipman, David Berkowitz, Edmund Kemper, Aileen Wuornos, you name it, they've all run out of steam sooner or later. This won't be any different. The Violet Killer will slip up or otherwise be brought down by good old-fashioned police work." Dylan firmly believed this as he sliced up his pancakes. Never mind the few serial killers, such as Jack the Ripper, who may have successfully eluded authorities before modern technology and forensic science took away their natural advantages. The Violet Killer serial madman would not have a long shelf life. They would see to it.

"So, what's with you and Special Agent Stabler?" Naomi tossed out casually, as she sipped coffee from her mug.

Dylan lifted a brow. "Excuse me?"

"You two seem to have hit it off."

"Yeah, I guess we have, if you're referring to a solid working relationship." He stared at her, sensing that she was implying something of a sexual nature. Was she actually jealous of the FBI profiler? "Other than that, I can assure you that it's strictly professional. Word has it that she's involved with another agent. Besides that, Agent Stabler is not my type."

"Oh." Naomi sipped her coffee and looked embarrassed that she had chosen to go down that road, indicating that she was still interested in him, romantically speaking. This gave Dylan the opening to satisfy his own curiosity on that theme, once and for all.

"What about you?" He forked a stack of pancakes. "Have you left some Secret Service agent or other lucky guy hanging while you're away?"

She batted her lashes. "If you're asking if I'm seeing someone, the answer is no. I've probably gone out on maybe two dates since arriving in Miami—and both proved to be disastrous, truthfully." Naomi met his eyes soulfully. "Guess it's not as easy to move on as I'd imagined."

Dylan's brows lowered. "Did you really think it would be?"

"I don't know what I thought." She ran a hand

through her hair edgily. "I just didn't want things to be any harder than they were in leaving. I know I made sacrifices and have to live with that." Naomi picked up her mug and tasted the coffee thoughtfully.

"We've both made sacrifices," Dylan acknowledged considerately. "That's part of life. We deal with it and try not to look back at the what-ifs too much." He only wished he had practiced more what he was now preaching. It was hard not to imagine the life they could have had. But seeing how well Naomi had done in her life after relocating, wishing she had stayed in Pebble Creek was being unfair to her. And him.

They ate in silence for a few minutes, as though weighing whether or not to say anything that might shatter the tentative truce in their understanding.

Finally, after wiping her mouth with a napkin, Naomi said coolly, "I plan to meet with Agent Stabler."

"Oh..." Dylan looked at her, wondering if this was still about something going on between him and the FBI agent that Naomi needed to ascertain for herself, before considering any possibility of repairing their own fractured relationship.

"Yes, she invited me at Uncle Roger's funeral to reach out to her, if I wanted to talk." Naomi took a hesitant breath. "Guess I would like to pick her brain in trying to gain more insight into this Violet Killer. Might help me to better come to terms with the type of perp he is and what my uncle may have been able to pick up in identifying him."

Dylan weighed whether or not he thought that was a good idea for Naomi to get more deeply vested in the case. Wouldn't that make it tougher to deal with Roger's loss? Or would it make it easier to digest while, at the same time, enabling her to tap into Patricia's expertise in characterizing the unsub as a big step in ultimately bringing him to justice? Maybe it could also be a way for him and Naomi to reactivate what they once meant to each other.

"Go for it," he told her with a straight look. "Agent Stabler definitely knows her stuff and has been a real asset in this investigation. Hope she can give you what you need."

Naomi smiled. "Thanks for your support, Dylan."

"No matter what, that's something you can always count on," he told her, grinning back, and meaning every word.

Chapter Nine

That afternoon, Naomi arranged to meet Patricia Stabler for coffee at the Java & Tea Corner on Willow Road. She wasn't sure if the FBI profiler would agree to a Sunday get-together, but it proved to be no problem. Indeed, for some reason, the special agent seemed just as eager to talk as Naomi. She rose from the side table to greet the gorgeous redhead, whom Naomi felt relieved that Dylan had no romantic interest in, in spite of the undetermined nature of their own relationship at the moment. "Hi," Naomi said awkwardly, noting that her pixie hair had even more volume as if freshly styled. Naomi's had put her own hair into a high ponytail.

"Hey." Patricia, who was casually dressed and wearing flats, smiled. She held out a thin-fingered hand in a professional motion, which Naomi shook. "Good to hear from you, Ms. Lincoln."

"Please, call me Naomi," she insisted, "Agent Stabler."

"Only if you'll call me Patricia."

"You're on." Naomi smiled sideways. "Shall we sit?"

"Sure." Patricia tossed her handbag on a corner of the table and sat across from her. Naomi was sure the FBI agent was packing. What one wasn't? Though, at times, feeling naked without her own weapon—especially in the tense environment she found herself in—Naomi had chosen to keep her firearm under lock and key at Dylan's place for this occasion, knowing that Patricia would have her back, should trouble arise.

They ordered espressos and pecan scones, after which Patricia nibbled on a scone and, peering at her, asked directly, "How are you doing, Naomi?"

She thought of giving the pat answer of good or fine, but given that she had taken the profiler up on her offer to talk about what was going on, that would obviously not hold up very well. So, instead, Naomi looked her in the eye and spoke truthfully. "I'm having trouble dealing with the fact that Sandra Neville's murder may have been meant as a warning to me by the Violet Killer that my turn is coming…"

Patricia's eyes grew wide. "What makes you think that?"

Naomi took out her cell phone, brought up the alarming text message and showed it to her.

"Seems like he wanted to get my attention." Naomi sucked in a deep breath. "And it worked."

"Hmm…" Patricia said musingly, gazing at the small screen. "I'd heard that he had texted you previously. But this is definitely taking it to another level."

Naomi concurred. "Since my uncle was murdered, I get the impression that the unsub has somehow latched onto me for some sick game—or worse—in the aftermath. Not sure if he's just getting some perverse thrill out of toying with the niece of the private investigator he gunned down, or what." She paused again, tasting the coffee. "Maybe you can shed some light on this—"

"I can try," the profiler indicated, sipping her own drink ponderingly. "From what I understand, you were never able to get any type of visual of the unsub on your laptop when he shot Roger, correct?"

"Correct. Just his shadow." Naomi shuddered at the thought. "If I'd only had some sort of inkling of what was about to happen, I could've at least warned my uncle, to give him a fighting chance."

"There was nothing you could have done." Patricia's tone rang with sympathy. "The unsub has become skilled in his modus operandi over the course of his killings. He wasn't about to break that pattern by revealing himself to you through a computer screen. That close call notwithstanding, you apparently got his attention in moving forward."

"How so?" Naomi tried to get into the unsub's head while grabbing a scone off the plate and taking a generous bite of it.

"My assessment of the man we're dealing with here is that he sees you as a sort of extension of Roger Lincoln, whom he viewed as a serious threat to exposing him. Being privy to info he took off your uncle's laptop—including perhaps that you're a Secret Service agent—the unsub, with his arrogance and proclivity for pushing the envelope, simply couldn't resist taunting you as a way to get under not only your skin, but that of the entire Task Force hunting for him." Patricia tilted her face. "Does that make sense?"

"Yes," Naomi answered, even as she tried to comprehend it in her head.

"As for Sandra Neville's death," Patricia pointed out, "she may or may not have been targeted because of her race, but it's more likely that she was targeted because of her routine and the unsub's risk assessment. Being African American was probably more happenstance, though certainly something that was apropos in his evil mind." She reached across the table and touched Naomi's hand. "So don't beat yourself up about Ms. Neville's misfortune. It is no more on you than the Violet Killer's other female victims."

Naomi nodded, feeling some comfort in her words as a criminal profiler. Still, she needed to get a better read on the serial killer if she was to more properly come to grips with his actions—and maybe what was yet to come. She took another bite of the scone, then asked, "What else can you tell me about the perp, aside from the fact that he goes after young, attractive women? What makes him tick?"

"I'm actually asked that a lot." Patricia sat back, contemplating the questions calmly. "Where do I start?" She sipped the espresso. "Most serial killers we hear about are sexually motivated in their actions, be it rape, torture, mutilation, cannibalism or some combo before death, or afterward. Fred West, Jeffrey Dahmer, Richard Ramirez and Dean Corll come to mind. Well, not the unsub. He does not sexually assault his victims—an important distinction from the aforementioned—but does strangle them to death, while leaving no DNA that can be traced back to him. This is not to say that he doesn't receive some type of gratification akin to sexual from his killings. And whether or not he was the victim of child sexual abuse is another question that can only be answered once he's identified."

Patricia grabbed another scone, holding it as if a prop. "As to what makes him tick, I would say it's the thrill of the kill. It turns him on to know he has the power of life and death over his chosen victims, and is not afraid to use it whenever the opportunity presents itself." She bit into the scone. "There's a predatory nature to the unsub, in which the killings have become somewhat of a sport for him in hunting for females who fit the characteristics that capture his fancy. So, that pretty much sums up the Violet Killer, other than the fact that, like other serial murderers, he aims to continue his work while avoiding capture at all costs."

"Interesting…" Naomi swallowed thickly as she contemplated the lengths the unsub was willing to go to in order to avoid capture, such as taking the life of her uncle Roger along with anyone else who stood in his way. Including her, Dylan and the criminal profiler sitting across from her. "Is there any significance to leaving the violet as his calling card?" she wondered curiously.

Patricia licked her lips. "In my experience, there is no significance in criminals' calling cards, per se, other than to keep law enforcement guessing and off balance." She wrinkled her nose. "If I were to stretch it here to try to make some sense of it, I'd say that the sweet aroma of the violets may emulate the tantalizing scent of a woman in the unsub's head, that fades with the victim's dying breath. But I wouldn't take that to the bank."

She chuckled humorlessly and Naomi pondered the notion, realizing she had been given a chilling crash course on the serial killer and like minds, making her uncomfortable. Still, at the same time, it made her feel better in having more to work with in sizing up the unsub who murdered eight women and her uncle. "Guess we both better stay away from violets," she said drily.

"You think?" Patricia rolled her eyes. She put the coffee mug to her mouth and gazed at Naomi thoughtfully. "I've heard some good things about you as a member of the US Secret Service."

"Did Dylan tell you that?" Naomi asked out of curiosity. Or was it more an assumption? Did their shoptalk include her as the subject matter?

"No," the FBI agent insisted. "I have my sources within the Secret Service. I wasn't prying. As you know, our agencies often work closely together in federal law enforcement. Your name came up when talking about the Violet Killer case that's made national headlines, including your uncle's involvement in the investigation."

"I see." Naomi wished she hadn't jumped the gun in practically feeling as though Dylan had crossed the line in his professional association and their personal relationship. Of course it had become common knowledge, even in Secret Service circles, that a serial killer was active in Pebble Creek, as would be the case for similar investigations around the country in the age of cable television and social media. The fact that it may not have risen to the level of a national security concern did not make it any less serious for law enforcement. "I do my best in carrying out the duties I've been assigned to do," she uttered humbly.

Patricia smiled. "So, when will you be heading back to Miami…?"

Naomi hedged over her mug. "I plan to stick around here for a little while," she confessed. "I've got some extra personal time, so…"

"Figured as much." The profiler gave her a perceptive look. "If I'm reading you correctly, in honor of your uncle, you would love to be on hand when we take the unsub down."

"Yes, ideally," Naomi acknowledged. In her heart of hearts, that would be the best way to give herself peace of mind. And allow her uncle Roger to rest in peace in his grave. But she also knew she couldn't put off returning to work forever. Especially since it had been more than two years since the killings began and the perp was still at large. Who was to say that he might not be continuing to murder women in Pebble Creek two years from now? "I'm not getting my hopes up that this will happen," she told her.

"Well, so long as you are in town and, undoubtedly, wanting to stay close to the investigation, you might as well make it official…"

Naomi cocked a brow. "Meaning…?"

Patricia leaned forward. "In representing the FBI as a key element of the Violet Killer Task Force, we'd love to have you on board as a sanctioned witness consultant in the case, just as Roger was. If you like, I can make this official request to the Secret Service. It may be a bit outside the norm, but given that you're an important witness to one of the Violet Killer's crimes, the first person on the scene of another murder attributed to him, and you're being taunted by the killer, it seems quite appropriate, under the circumstances."

"Yes, it does, doesn't it?" Naomi found herself in total agreement. She should be part of this criminal investigation into her uncle's murder, as well as those poor women who fell prey to this psychopath serial killer. Especially since the unsub seemed determined for some reason to draw her in like a spider in his web of strangulation deaths. But would her boss go for it? And would Dylan be on board?

Reading her thoughts, Patricia said, "If you need to run it by Dylan first or…"

"Let's do it!" Naomi practically shouted in a defensive manner, while wondering if Patricia thought they were a couple again. Had Dylan indicated anything of that nature? Either way, she didn't need his permission, even if Dylan was the lead detective on the local level in the investigation. Moreover, they had worked together in an official capacity before. Why should this be any different? "Put in the request and I'll clear it with my boss, Jared Falcony, who runs the Miami Field Office."

"Wonderful." Patricia flashed her teeth and raised her mug to toast. "With any luck, we'll catch the perp before you have to leave."

"I hope so." Naomi lifted her coffee and the two mugs clinked. Even then, the thought of going back to Miami and leaving Dylan behind again weighed on her. This, in spite of the fact that their relationship had ended two years ago and there was no real indication on Dylan's part that he wanted to start it back up. Well, there was that nostalgic kiss, that did more than stir up old memories. At least for her. Was this true for him also, his words to the contrary? Even so, she wondered as well if fantasies could go only so far as she recalled the dream last night in which they made love like it still meant something to them in the real world. Maybe it did.

STANDING ON HIS DECK, a beer in hand, Dylan was admittedly curious as to how the coffee meeting between Naomi and Patricia went. He imagined the two women, both strong and independent, got along well and could even become friends once this case was over and they went back to their respective jobs with the foremost federal law enforcement agencies. There was also reason to believe that in her expertise as a criminal profiler, Patricia could certainly be helpful in giving Naomi some real perspective on the Violet Killer, in characterizing him and trying to anticipate his next move. On the other hand, Naomi, as an eyewitness to Roger's murder and the one who discovered Sandra Neville's body, was just as valuable in what she brought to the table. That, along with her being an equal in her role with the Secret Service, had to appeal to the FBI agent in her determination to bring the unsub to his knees before long.

As far as he was concerned, Dylan had no problem with Naomi reaching out to a key member of the Task Force, if it meant helping her to get through this ordeal as best she could. They were all dealing with it in their own ways, and he was no exception. Watching young women in the community die so senselessly, with their whole lives ahead of them, put a definite strain on his ability to separate the daily grind of police work from the harsh realities of life and death. It played with his psyche and he didn't like it one bit. The only true way to return to some sense of normalcy was to put an end to this reign of terror.

When he saw Naomi drive up, Dylan's heart skipped a beat for some reason. He wasn't sure if it was in anticipation for what she had to say or the sheer joy of knowing she had made it back safe and sound, with a serial killer out there seeking an opportunity to isolate her. Whatever the case, Dylan couldn't help but feel relief as Naomi got out of the SUV and headed toward the deck.

"Hey," he said evenly, greeting her.

"Hey." Her tone was unreadable, but she offered him a smile, as if for what came next.

"How did it go?"

She took the beer bottle from him and took a generous drink, before handing it back. "Why don't we talk about it inside?"

"Okay." Dylan followed her through the door, his interest piqued.

Chapter Ten

"So, here's the thing," Naomi began, pacing the room as though she had lost something. "Special Agent Stabler and I—actually, it was her suggestion—thought it might be a good idea for me to become a temporary member of the Violet Killer Task Force, as an official Secret Service agent consultant."

"Oh, really?" Dylan's eyes danced with amusement, feeling somewhat relieved that Patricia hadn't tried to practically recruit her as an FBI agent. "Makes perfect sense to me."

She stopped pacing, staring at him. "Seriously?"

"Of course. Did you think I would try to pull rank on the special agent, as if I could, and shoot down her idea?" He lowered his chin. "Well...?"

Naomi fluttered her lashes. "Truthfully, I assumed—and even Agent Stabler—that you might balk at the idea, not to pull rank, but as your way of pushing back on my greater involvement in order to protect me from the unsub."

Dylan stepped closer to her. It was true that he would do anything to keep her safe. Roger would expect no less of him. But it was just as true that he knew from firsthand experience that when Naomi put her mind to something, there was little he could do to stop her. So why try? Especially when her unique position in the scheme of things made her continued presence helpful in the investigation. He understood her need, under the circumstances, to hang around for as long as she could to try to help nab the perp, if at all possible. "So, your boss is on board with this?" Dylan didn't imagine that she could have an open-ended sabbatical from her official duties with the Secret Service, no matter how many strings Patricia managed to pull in that regard.

"Haven't run it by him yet," admitted Naomi, wringing her hands. "But, since Patricia, er, Agent Stabler, will be making the request as a key FBI point person in the investigation, I don't imagine it will be a problem."

Dylan grinned. "Then it won't be with me," he assured her and took a sip from his beer bottle. Part of him loved the idea of working with her in an official capacity again. Another part welcomed the idea of her staying in Pebble Creek for as long as possible, as he couldn't help but enjoy being around his onetime love. Still, the longer she was in town, the more at risk Naomi was for being in the Violet Killer's realm. Meaning, she would need to remain vigilant at all times. He delivered that wisdom to her in a caring tone.

"Yes, I'll keep eyes in the back of my head for any signs of the unsub approaching." Naomi regarded

Dylan with a straight face. "Seriously, I won't know-ingly put myself in danger. Or give him an easy way to attack. But I won't run and hide like a mouse from an alley cat, either."

"Never thought you would," he made clear. After all, it was the fighter in Naomi that had attracted him in the first place. Once he got past her hot looks and sexy body. And her totally appealing personality.

"Glad to hear that." She moved right up to him and, once again, took the beer and drank some. He had never known her to be much of a beer drinker, but he didn't mind sharing the bottle. "Oh, there is one other thing…" she teased him.

"What might that be?" he was almost afraid to ask, and eager to hear at the same time.

"This…" Naomi cupped his cheeks, lowered his face and planted a firm kiss on Dylan's mouth. He was happy to kiss her back, tasting the beer off her mouth. The kiss continued for at least a full minute with neither making a move to pull away. Every part of Dylan's body was aflame with desire to carry this further, maybe all the way to his bed. Or hers. Did she feel the same way?

Using all the strength he had, Dylan broke away and peered into her eyes. "Is this another for-old-times'-sake moment between us?"

"Maybe." Naomi put a finger to her moist lips and blushed. "Or maybe it can be a for-new-times'-sake moment, if you're open to that possibility."

Those were words Dylan had dreamed of hearing from her inviting mouth for a long time. The possibility of resurrecting their love life was enticing beyond words. How could it not be? She was everything to him, and that had not changed over time. Or had it? But what exactly did she mean with the possibility for new times in a relationship? And were any such possibilities practical, given their circumstances in life after the Violet Killer case had long passed?

Now seemed like as good a time as any to say what had long been on his mind, sticking to it like glue as to what might have been. "I was going to ask you to marry me two years ago," he confessed.

Naomi's mouth opened to an imperfect O. "Why didn't you?" she asked, a catch to her voice.

"You know why." His lips pursed, believing it should have been obvious, even if unspoken at the time. "You told me about your plans with the Secret Service and relocating to the other side of the country. I wasn't about to make you choose between a dream job and me."

Her brows twitched. "Sounds like a copout to me, Dylan," she spoke bluntly. "If you weren't man enough to say what was on your mind, don't blame me for moving ahead with my own life. If you wanted to marry me, you should have asked!"

"Would it have made a difference?" He held her gaze, feeling his heart beating rapidly while wondering if he had indeed blown it, big-time, for all the wrong reasons.

Naomi sighed and turned away from him. "I have no idea," she indicated candidly. "Things were clicking between us then. I wanted more from you. I also wanted more for myself." She refaced him. "Had you proposed, it could have changed everything. Or not. I guess we'll never know."

"Yeah, guess not," he snorted, angry more at himself than anything. Why hadn't he been more courageous, instead of trying to do right by her and her ambitions, and just let the chips fall where they may? Had he done so, they might be husband and wife today, with a child on the way. Instead of two single people who had missed their moment in the sun. Or was it not too late to turn the ship around and recapture what they lost?

"I'm going to go take a shower," Naomi cut into his reverie with a sharp tone. "And, no, it's not an invitation to join me, Dylan. I think a kiss is enough for today. Maybe that's as far as this was meant to go. After all, throwing caution to the wind doesn't seem to be in your DNA in matters of the heart."

Dylan stood there flatfooted and speechless as she sashayed away, feeling as though he had let the best thing to ever happen to him slip from his grasp. Again.

HAD SHE OVERREACTED? Cast blame where there was none? Or maybe made him the heavy to make herself feel better in going to work for the Secret Service when she could have been Mrs. Dylan Hester. This weighed heavily on Naomi's mind the next day as she went out for a morning swim in the warm waters of Pebble Creek Lake all by her lonesome. Last night, she and Dylan barely said two words to one another while eating leftover pizza from the night before. It was as if each was afraid of saying something that might put the other off. For her part, she was still trying to come to grips with the missed opportunity of the proposal that never happened. Had Dylan confided in Uncle Roger about it? Had he encouraged him to step aside and allow her career to blossom? Or had Dylan decided all on his own that he would use her news as a convenient excuse to back down from a legal future together? All the more frustrating to Naomi was that she loved her job with the Secret Service and couldn't imagine being deprived of the opportunity. As such, could she really blame Dylan for not standing in the way of such an achievement and the personal growth to accompany it?

Casting aside the self-pity, confusion and second thoughts, Naomi swam the freestyle stroke, something she had been doing since childhood. She had perfected it and become just as proficient with the backstroke and breaststroke while swimming often in the alluring waters of Miami Beach. It was no less enjoyable in Pebble Creek Lake, even if she was in a crappy mood. Dylan had left early for work without them seeing each other, having retired to their separate rooms for bed. She would give him his space and he was willing to give Naomi hers. But that could last for only so long, since she was still living in his cabin. While she was in town, they would need to work together to some degree toward a common goal of solving her uncle's murder and other homicides attributed to the Violet Killer. Whether she and Dylan could remain on friendly terms or more than friends beyond that was another matter altogether.

As she homed in on her surroundings, Naomi realized that she had swum farther away from the waters close to Dylan's cabin than she had intended. She scanned the shoreline, where there were other lakefront houses and condos, reflecting the popularity of the area and boom in construction. For whatever reason, Naomi had the feeling she was being watched. But by whom? She noted a speedboat from a distance. There was a man on board who seemed to be looking in her direction. Was she just being paranoid? She turned back to the coast. Only now did she notice the tall man, wearing a dark cap and dark clothing. He was standing on grass, looking through binoculars—at her! Was he merely checking out the gorgeous scenery, with her as an added attraction? Or were his motives more sinister?

Naomi felt a chill at the thought that the man might be the Violet Killer, sizing her up for the strangulation kill. Were that the case, he was also making it clear that he knew her whereabouts and was coming for her. Her heart racing, she started to swim away from the man and toward the cabin. She almost expected him to jump into the water and come after her. With powerful legs and sheer determination, perhaps he could catch up to her and drown her, even if she put up a good fight. Using her own skills in the water, Naomi picked up the pace, determined not to let her life end at the hands of a demented killer. When she approached the shoreline, she darted her eyes in the direction where the man had been standing, fearful that he had already kept up with her and would be waiting for her to come ashore. But she saw no one. He had vanished practically into thin air. Or had he been there at all? Had she only seen what she wanted to?

Doubting her own eyes, Naomi climbed out of the water, her one-piece floral bathing suit clinging to her like a second skin. She grabbed a microfiber beach towel from the grass and ran across it in a hurry as if her life depended on it. Once inside, she made sure the doors and windows were locked and reactivated the outdoor motion detectors to alert her to any possible intruder approaching the cabin. A gaze through the window wall gave no indication that someone was out there. Still, her instincts were going crazy with concern. She scaled the stairs and went into Dylan's office. Cutting on his laptop, she pulled up the quad split screen to check out the multiple security cameras on the property, catching every point of entry. There were no signs of activity. Could the unsub have somehow outsmarted the surveillance system, waiting to strike once she let her guard down?

Not taking any chances, Naomi ran into her room, where she opened a bottom dresser drawer and removed the locked container holding her loaded Glock. She took it out and readied herself, should she need to use it in self-defense. It was suddenly as quiet as a mouse in there. She moved stealthily out of the room, down the hall and back to the first floor, eyes darting for anything that moved. Nothing.

Lowering her weapon, Naomi breathed in a sigh of relief, while wishing that Dylan would walk through that front door as an added means of re-assurance. No one was after her. At least not this day. She wondered when it was that she became so easily spooked. Had witnessing the execution of her uncle and finding a dead woman been enough to cause her to lose confidence in herself? If so, how did she get it back even while feeling vulnerable? These troubling thoughts were interrupted as Naomi heard her cell phone ring. Was it another threatening text message from the unsub? Once again, her heart skipped a beat. She walked to the kitchen island, where she had left the phone, and lifted it in expectation. There was a text. Only it was from her boss, Jared Falcony. He had approved the request for her to be on temporary loan to the Violet Killer Task Force for anything she could bring to the table in solving the murder of Roger Lincoln and related homicides.

DYLAN RODE WITH Gregory Hwang to the crime lab, where there was news on DNA and other forensic evidence collected in connection with the murder of Sandra Neville. Both detectives hoped this might be the break they were waiting for in identifying a suspect in her murder.

"As yet, we have no new leads on anyone who may have been at the scene of the crime at the time it occurred," Hwang muttered from behind the wheel. "Surveillance cameras around the wooded area have not turned up anything we can put a finger on in the investigation."

"What about the search volunteers?" questioned Dylan from the passenger seat. "Anyone stand out as suspicious?"

"Not really. Some were wishy-washy on why they were there at all, as if it was just to hang out with people. So far, everyone we've interviewed has an alibi for at least one of the killings attributed to the Violet Killer."

This didn't surprise Dylan. His own assessment of those in Naomi's circle of volunteers was that they were truly dedicated to finding the missing woman alive and seemed genuinely shaken up that it didn't turn out that way. He suspected that the unsub was spying on Naomi from a safe distance to allow for a quick getaway. Speaking of getaway vehicles, it made Dylan think about the dark-colored SUV Naomi thought had an aggressive driver in it—possibly the Violet Killer—in putting the fear in her. "Anything on that SUV we're looking for?" Dylan asked Hwang, knowing they had already eliminated it as being owned by one of their current suspects.

"We're still trying to track it down," he answered woefully. "Turns out, we have more than our fair share of dark SUVs registered in the county. It's a long shot, but we may be able to break it down to a few that were possibly on that street at that time."

Dylan nodded to that effect. He was still not entirely convinced that the SUV incident was actually connected to their serial killer investigation. But if

Naomi felt threatened enough to make it an issue, they were going to take it seriously. While this definitely commanded his attention, he found himself drifting back to the spat, if it could be called that, with Naomi yesterday after her get-together with Patricia Stabler. Dylan had known from the moment he did it that he had put his large foot in his mouth when he brought up the marriage proposal that he never gave Naomi. Why couldn't he have just left well enough alone and not said anything? Didn't they have enough on their plate without complicating things further between them? If he had wanted to drive her out of his cabin and back to the house she had inherited from Roger, Dylan couldn't have made it any easier. All he could do now was hope he hadn't blown things altogether and they could get past this and keep her safe till the unsub was caught. Or Naomi had decided it was taking too long and headed back to Miami. Admittedly, the idea that he could still sweep her off her feet was something he was happy to entertain. Could he really let her go again when the kisses they shared told him that the old magic and chemistry between them was still alive and well? Or was he deluding himself in thinking he could repair something that may well be unfixable at this stage?

"You've gone quiet on me over there, Hester," Hwang commented from behind the wheel of his department-issued sedan. "What's up?"

Dylan bared his soul to him, feeling the need to unload. "Naomi and I have shared a couple of kisses since she's been back in Pebble Creek," he confessed. "I told her I wanted to propose two years ago, but didn't want to step on the toes of her new career with the Secret Service. That went well." He made a sarcastic groan. "She somehow turned it around on me and accused me of essentially not stepping up to the plate when I had my chance. I could hardly push back against that. Maybe I did blow it and will have to live with the decision I made for what I thought were the right reasons." Dylan sighed and gazed out the window. "The last thing I wanted to do was make things uncomfortable for her while she's staying with me. Especially when a serial killer is still on the prowl around town."

"Wow!" Hwang expressed in an empathetic tone. "Looks like you've really put yourself in a jam."

"You think?" Dylan rolled his eyes sarcastically.

"Doesn't mean it's a box you can't climb out of, Dylan. Talk to her, man."

"I've tried that and it didn't get me very far."

"So, try again until it does," Hwang pressed. "If you still love her, and I'm sensing that you do, then you need to find out if she feels the same way. Then try to fix things. If what you had is still meant to be, don't let distance, figuratively and literally, stand in your way. Once this case is over, maybe you need to consider relocation, if that's what it takes. I hear that the Miami Police Department is always looking for great detectives. That way, you'd be within shouting distance of the Secret Service field office there. I'm just saying."

"I hear you," Dylan said, shocked at the suggestion that he quit the force. He tried to imagine giving up his job as a senior detective to start over elsewhere. If Naomi did it, why couldn't he? But would that even be enough to prove his love and win her back? Or had he burned his bridges to her heart?

"Second chances, if this is one of them, don't come around every day," Hwang pointed out with an edge to his voice. "I should know."

Dylan took in his honest words. He knew that Hwang had lost his wife to divorce three years ago, leaving him to care for their twin daughters. A good father, Hwang still pined for his ex, hoping she might someday walk back into his life. Dylan wanted the same thing with Naomi, when he got right down to it. But wanting something and being able to make it happen were two entirely different things.

Chapter Eleven

"I've got some positive news for you guys," George Suina said almost jubilantly as the forensic science technician greeted Dylan and Hwang at his workstation in the crime lab.

"We could sure use some," Hwang moaned dramatically.

"Yeah," agreed Dylan, while withholding judgment.

"All right." Suina pinched his nose. "Why don't we get on with it, then. We removed DNA from under the nails of Sandra Neville that wasn't her own. It almost certainly came from the person who attacked Ms. Neville in her struggle for survival, which unfortunately came up short. But she gave us something to work with in developing a forensic profile of the suspected perp. We're using the FBI's Combined DNA Index System, or CODIS, to see if there is a DNA match within its Convicted Offender and Arrestee Indices that can be linked to other serial violent offenses and/or known offenders. If our unsub is anywhere in the system, this will flush him out."

"That is huge," Dylan admitted with optimism. Having what would amount to their first potential DNA profile of the unsub might be just what they needed to break this case wide open. Assuming he had left behind other DNA during the commission of crimes.

"Yeah, I agree," said Hwang. "So, how long are you going to keep us hanging before we have some results?"

"Never soon enough, right?" Suina grinned glibly. "The labs are pretty busy these days, as you know. But serial killer cases, such as the Violet Killer, get priority. You'll know as soon as I do if there is a hit."

Dylan wrinkled his nose, sharing in Hwang's impatience. Still, this was a step in the right direction, so best to take it for what it was worth. "Anything else?" he asked the analyst.

"As a matter of fact, there is," Suina voiced teasingly. He turned on his monitor and they saw a digital image of a footprint. "Crime scene technicians came across a shoeprint beneath the undergrowth where Sandra Neville's remains were discovered. We believe the footwear outsole impression of a size-ten right shoe may have come from the unsub during the process of subduing and killing the victim. Of course, someone else could have left the footprint some other time. We can rule out it belonging to Ms. Neville, whose feet were measured at size eight."

"Was it an athletic shoe, dress shoe or what?" Hwang asked.

"That's still a work in progress," Suina bemoaned.

"We'll work as hard as we can to try to come up with the manufacturer, brand name and any distinctive pattern that you can work with as possible forensic footwear evidence in trying to nail the perp."

"Let us know when, and if, you come up with anything pertinent," Dylan told him.

Suina patted him on the shoulder. "You bet."

Outside, Hwang faced Dylan. "Think the DNA belongs to our unsub?"

"You have a better answer?" Dylan challenged him.

"Not really."

"Neither do I. Let's just wait and see if we have a match and go from there."

"Yeah." Hwang bobbed his head.

Dylan's cell phone buzzed. He took it out of his pocket and saw it was a text from Naomi. She believed it was a distinct possibility that someone had been watching her while she was swimming in the lake.

Having replaced her swimsuit with a blouse and slim ankle pants, while putting her feet into some espadrille slip-ons, Naomi waited anxiously for Dylan to return to the cabin. When he did, she nearly ran into his arms, knowing they would protect her. But she held back, not wanting to mix the emotions of their past relationship with the confusion about where things stood right now. Besides that, there were more pertinent things to focus on that required some degree of professionalism, with a killer possibly stalking her.

"Are you all right?" Dylan's deep voice illustrated the strain in his features.

"Yes," Naomi told him, having shut off the motion sensor alarm for outdoors when she saw him coming.

He stepped closer, inspecting her, as if to be sure. "Tell me what you saw and where while swimming."

She gathered herself, running a hand through hair still wet from the water. "Well, I had gone out and drifted south, away from the lake frontage of your cabin," she explained. "I suddenly had a sense that someone was watching me. That's when I saw a man standing on the grass with binoculars aimed straight at me."

"You're sure he wasn't just checking out the lake?" Dylan flashed her a questioning look.

Naomi batted her lashes. "If you're asking me if I could swear that he was homed in on me, I would say no. But given there was no one else in sight, other than a boat that was too far out, it seemed like a reasonable conclusion." Even if one she herself questioned. "In any event, I didn't want to stick around and see what happened next. So, I swam back to shore as fast as I could and went into the cabin. I checked the security video cameras on your laptop around the perimeter of the property and saw nothing unusual. Still, it was something I thought you should know." She neglected to mention that she also grabbed her firearm to be on the safe side.

"What did the man look like?" Dylan asked evenly.

"He was tall and wore a dark cap to go with dark

clothing. I was afraid when I got back on land that he would be there waiting for me. But there was no sign of him, including where I first spotted him." She smoothed an eyebrow. "Maybe he was just binocular gazing and I happened to come into his view," she speculated, wondering if it was a good idea to scare Dylan into thinking she was in trouble.

"Or maybe you were on to something in that you were being watched," he said thoughtfully. "Care to take a walk with me so you can show me where you first saw this man?"

"Yes." She gave him a tiny smile, belying the tension between them that was thick as fog.

Outside, they walked across the grass toward the lake and then followed the bends and curves of the shoreline that took them in the direction where Naomi knew the man had been standing. At one point, her shoulder brushed against Dylan's hard body and the sensations echoed through her. Had he sensed this? Or even felt the same?

"Look, about yesterday—" Dylan gazed at her, as if to break the spell he had over her bodily reaction to him. "I was out of line in bringing up something that was best left in the past where it belonged."

"I'm the one who should be apologizing," Naomi said sincerely, in owning up to her own role in their confrontation. "You had every right to say what was on your mind."

"Really?" He made a humming sound of disagreement. "I never intended to make you uncomfortable."

"You didn't." She saw no reason to guilt-trip him.

But she did think it appropriate to be honest at the same time. "You should have said what was on your mind two years ago, Dylan. After what we had, you owed me that much, regardless of how I might have responded."

"You're absolutely right," he said. "I was bone-headed when thinking that by proposing, I would only be putting you on the spot and possibly standing in your way. I should have manned up and just put it out there, giving you the option to make your own fully informed choice, one way or the other, and let the chips fall where they may..."

Naomi was happy to hear him say that. Even if saddened that she never got the chance to say she would marry him, probably on the spot in the way she felt about him. Whether that meant she would have still wanted to go to Miami or not, she honestly couldn't say one way or the other. At least now they had cleared the air and could be friends, if nothing else. Or so she hoped. "Can we just start over?" she asked tentatively, unsure what that meant exactly. Or if he was ready to do that, beyond a working relationship.

Dylan's eyes crinkled when he smiled. "I'd like that very much."

"Me, too." She smiled back at him, wondering if there was still a chance that romance might blossom between them. When they reached a certain area, Naomi stopped and studied the lake and distance from where she believed she was swimming. "I think he was standing around here."

Dylan peered at the water for a long moment. Then he began looking at the grass and took a few hesitant steps, as if trying to avoid a land mine. He halted, staring at what looked to Naomi to be an impression that could come only from a shoe. He knelt and studied it further.

"What is it?" she asked curiously. "You think he left that…?"

"Maybe." Dylan stood up and favored her with an indistinct expression. "Seems like it could be a size ten…"

She lifted a brow. "I don't follow."

"There was a size-ten shoeprint found near the spot where you discovered Sandra Neville's body," Dylan explained. "It was obscured by the underbrush. Forensic specialists believe it may have been left there unintentionally by her killer. If the man you saw is one and the same, he could have been wearing the same pair of shoes and, unbeknownst to him, provided us an important clue—make that two clues—in identifying him."

"Wow." Naomi was excited at the possibility, but this quickly lessened as reality hit like running into a door. "It's a long shot that this footprint belongs to the man who was watching me."

"Yeah, it is," Dylan admitted, careful not to step on the print that was so close to the water it was almost as though the person standing there was itching to jump in. Possibly to come after her. "But it could also be a rare slipup by the unsub that can only work to our advantage." Dylan pulled out his cell and took a few pictures of the shoeprint from various angles and lengths. Afterward, he made a call. "Hey, George, I'm sending you some photos of a shoeprint left by the lake, not far from my cabin. I'd like you to compare it to the digital footprint taken from the Sandra Neville crime scene and see if they could possibly have come from the same shoe. Make it ASAP. Oh, and let's get someone over here to collect any potential forensic evidence, doing it by the book, in case it belongs to our unsub."

Naomi watched Dylan taking charge in not wanting to provide any loopholes that any good lawyer could exploit, should it come to that. It was one reason that she had become attracted to the detective initially, in working for and alongside her uncle Roger. It led to other reasons for that attraction that would turn into love. A love, she knew deep down in her soul, that had never died and was alive and well, in spite of them moving in different directions. Or was she actually the only one guilty of turning her back on what they had?

"A CELL PHONE and laptop were found in a dumpster. We think they may belong to Roger," Dylan informed Naomi the next day, after getting off the phone. They had just finished eating breakfast and seemed to be getting along again, having gotten past a few hiccups in their relationship. Or whatever he wanted to call what was going on between them. He was curious as to where she stood on the subject, but now was not the time to get into that.

"Who found them?" Naomi asked curiously as they stood on the deck.

"Apparently, a homeless man was digging around in it for food or who knows what. A uniformed officer, Carol Newton, spotted him holding a garbage bag and checked it out. Seeing the items inside, she immediately became suspicious and turned them over to forensics. Could be a false lead." Dylan sighed. "Or it may be the break we needed to uncover important information in your uncle's death and break the case wide open." He wasn't getting his hopes up and Dylan certainly didn't want Naomi to get too excited, either. But it was a possible development that needed to be investigated, along with other leads they were pursuing. "I'm on my way to the crime lab to see if they've come up with anything."

"I'd like to come, too." Naomi looked at him intently. "Now that I'm part of the Violet Killer Task Force for the time being, I'd like to be kept in the loop on any serious movement in the case."

Dylan had no real reason to deny her this request. Especially as the Secret Service, FBI and even the Pebble Creek PD were all on board, believing that Naomi could be a real asset as the only living witness to at least one of the homicides attributed to the unsub. "Understood," Dylan said in an agreeable tone. "Let's go."

She gave a satisfied smile. "I'm ready."

Fifteen minutes later, they were in the crime laboratory, where digital forensic analyst Tabitha McKinnon was with Agent Patricia Stabler.

"Hey, you two," Patricia hummed, making Dylan wonder if she thought they were a couple again. Or was that more wishful thinking on his part?

"Hey," he said to the profiler.

"Agent Stabler," Naomi spoke formally to her. "Hi, Tabitha."

"Naomi," the analyst greeted her unemotionally from her workstation.

"Looks like we're all here for the same reason," remarked Patricia. "Tabitha was just about to enlighten me on where things stood."

Dylan faced Tabitha. "I understand you have a cell phone and laptop," he said tonelessly.

"Yeah, we have them," Tabitha confirmed. "Both items appear to have been worked over pretty good by someone who obviously didn't want what was on them to be recovered."

"Have you determined if they belong to my uncle Roger?" Naomi asked eagerly.

"We were able to remove partial prints from the phone and laptop that matched Roger's prints on file," Tabitha announced triumphantly. She pulled open a drawer and slid out a shelf. On it were a bagged cell phone and laptop. "Apparently, the unsub had no problem with the possibility that we might retrieve the items and link them to Roger. It was as though the perp wanted to rub it in our faces as something he could get away with, as if untouchable."

Dylan noted that Naomi looked to be unstable on her feet. For an instant, he feared he may have to catch her before her legs collapsed. Patricia picked up on it, too, grabbing her arm, then asking: "Are you okay?"

Naomi steadied herself. "I'm fine. Just seeing the laptop that my uncle was using when we…" She paused. "Anyway, I hope it provides some answers."

"Don't we all," seconded Patricia.

Dylan followed up on that. "Were you able to get any information from the cell or laptop?" he asked the forensic examiner.

"The cell phone, yes," Tabitha answered and frowned. "No such luck with the laptop, I'm afraid."

"Tell us what you have from the phone," pressed Patricia, peering at her.

"All right." Tabitha turned on her monitor, where they saw a digital image of a cell phone. "Since Roger's cell phone was locked and has a fingerprint scanner, in order to get inside with no password option, we had to use specialized software to mimic what turned out to be his thumbprint. We were able to take a high-resolution image of the print in our system to create a 3D-printed mold. Worked like a charm to unlock it!" A series of phone numbers appeared on the monitor. "We're still going through it, but these were the calls Roger made in the days leading up to his death. Do any of them ring a bell, Naomi?"

Staring at the screen, she responded thoughtfully, "Yes, my own number is there. Not sure about the rest. Probably client contacts and…leads…" She choked back the words. "At least one number was probably a woman my uncle had been seeing. Her name's Brenda Quinlan."

"We'll check it out," Tabitha promised evenly.

Dylan doubted that Roger's girlfriend played any role in his death, but they would not rule out anyone. Or leave any stones unturned in getting to the truth and the culprit. "What about his laptop?" he asked, recalling her disillusion there. "Anything at all?" He imagined that the unsub destroyed any info it contained before discarding the laptop.

"Zilch." Tabitha's lips twisted. She walked to the shelf with Roger's damaged computer. "Whoever dumped the laptop scrubbed it of all files, making recovery all but impossible. Still, there are ways in which we may be able to retrieve at least some of the so-called lost information. But that will take time."

"Time we don't have," groaned Dylan, knowing every second counted in solving this case.

"Might I make a suggestion?" Naomi put forth, studying the laptop.

"Be our guest," Patricia responded interestedly.

"My colleague in the Secret Service, Agent Sophia Menendez, happens to be a whiz when it comes to computer and telecommunications fraud. Retrieving lost files, and quickly, is right up her alley." Naomi gazed at Dylan and Patricia. "Given the sense of urgency, if you like, I can give Sophia a call and have her take a look at the laptop."

"The FBI would certainly have no problem with that," Patricia said. "We know the Secret Service is on par with our agency in investigating computer crimes. If Agent Menendez is able and willing to take a crack at it, why not?"

"You'll get no argument from me there," Tabitha agreed. "This isn't about fighting over who should get the first dibs in outwitting the system cleaner. We all just want to solve this case by any means necessary."

Dylan was inclined to concur with all of them. He trusted Naomi. If she trusted her colleague to handle this in an expedited manner and with positive results, he certainly wouldn't stand in the way. "I'll need to clear it with Chief Frazier," he pointed out, "but as far as I'm concerned, it's a go." He nodded at Naomi. "Give her a call and let's get the ball rolling."

"Thank you." Naomi showed her teeth. "I'll call Agent Menendez right away."

Dylan smiled back, knowing this was something Naomi needed in contributing to the investigation into Roger's death. Any relevant info he left behind on the laptop couldn't come soon enough, especially since Roger hadn't bothered to back up any files on-line. Probably never thinking it would need to come down to that as a possible means in solving his death.

Chapter Twelve

Feeling empowered and a bit more settled after seeing her uncle Roger's laptop that represented the last conversation they ever had, Naomi went outside, where she could gather her thoughts before speaking to Sophia in private. It had been more difficult than she had expected to keep it together, after witnessing a murder and having the evidence of it practically stare back at her. Now the hope was that the unidentified person responsible would be exposed and brought to justice. This was her way of playing an important role in making that happen, thanks to Dylan, Patricia and Chief Frazier allowing Naomi to step outside the box in pursuit of findings that might still exist within a laptop, as if her uncle's final message from the grave.

She took out her cell phone and speed-dialed Sophia's number, practicing in her mind what Naomi wanted to say to her. When she appeared on the screen, Sophia was all smiles. "Well, hello, stranger…"

"Hey." Naomi smiled thinly. It hadn't been that long since they last talked, had it? "Do you have a sec?"

"Of course. Just got back to Miami and I'm already bored to death. Don't tell that to Jared Falcony, though. Otherwise, I might be sent for an assignment in Timbuktu."

"Speaking of Jared…" Naomi mentioned that he had approved her sticking around Pebble Creek for a bit longer in a consultant capacity. "Anything I can do to help find the Violet Killer."

"That perp gives me the creeps—in a Samuel Little kind of way," Sophia said, making a face in reference to the serial killer who was believed to have murdered dozens of women during his lifetime. "I'm glad to hear that you're helping out there. After what you witnessed, it's understandable you'd want to try to do right by your uncle and those poor women the unsub targeted."

On that note of support, Naomi cut right to the chase. "I need a big favor."

"Okay, sure. What's up?"

"They found Uncle Roger's laptop," explained Naomi. "It's been wiped clean. Meaning anything that he may have had in his files that could lead to the unsub has been erased. I was hoping that you could take a look at the laptop and see if anything can be recovered. I'll okay it with Jared, of course."

"I'd be happy to check it out." Sophia's eyes lit. "And Jared won't object," she spoke confidently. "He wants to see justice served in this case as much as I do. Can't make any promises, but this is in my repertoire. If there's a will—and there always is—I will do my best to find a way, no pun intended."

"Thank you." Naomi grinned, knowing she could count on her friend at crunch time. And vice versa.

"I'm guessing you need this like yesterday, instead of tomorrow?"

"You guessed right. The sooner we can see if there's anything there, the better."

"Got it," said Sophia. "Overnight the laptop to me and I'll get started right away."

"Will do." Knowing her friend, Naomi waited for Sophia to say what else was surely on her mind.

"So, what's happening with you and Detective Hester?"

"We're working our way through some issues," she said pensively. "Other than that, everything's fine."

"When you say *fine*, do you mean you're not tearing each other's hair out? Or are the embers starting to burn again?"

Naomi laughed. "You do have a way with words. No embers burning exactly, but we have had our moments," she had to admit.

"So, you're starting to have feelings for the man again?" persisted Sophia.

Naomi thought about it. Feelings? It went much deeper than that. Those kisses made that abundantly clear to her. "Not sure the feelings ever went away," she responded truthfully. "I'm just not sure what to do with them. Or if I should even try to make waves that he may not be ready for, bumpy waters and all."

"Do whatever you need to resolve unsettled issues, Naomi. Just be sure you don't get in over your head and end up hurt—or coming away with new regrets."

"I hear you, Sophia." Naomi colored. "I'll be careful," she promised her, not wishing to take a leap of faith only to fall overboard. On the other hand, romance was always a risky proposition. Was it not? Maybe seeing where things could go with Dylan wasn't such a bad idea. Till that proved to be the case.

When she hung up, Naomi saw Dylan standing there. He offered her a slow grin, making her wonder just how much of the conversation he had heard. She froze at the thought of trying to explain her words and meanings. "Hey," she uttered hesitantly.

"Hey." His expression was now unreadable, as if by design. "How did it go with your friend?"

"She's in." Naomi's cheeks rose gleefully. "Sophia's ready to see if she can reclaim Uncle Roger's deleted files. Or as many as possible."

"Good, because the chief is on board, too. Let's see if she can work some magic."

Naomi chuckled. "No pressure, right?"

Dylan grinned sidelong. "There's always pressure," he voiced thickly. "That's the nature of the beast called law enforcement that we're both sworn to. That can only be lessened when we can bring the Violet Killer case to a close."

This was something for which she could not offer a sarcastic comeback. The unsub had made sure of that. So long as her uncle's killer remained at large, there could be no letting up. Not till he was under lock and key. Or otherwise no longer a threat to society. Or her. "Agreed," Naomi told Dylan without a catch to her voice.

"THERE'S NEWS," Dylan informed Naomi an hour later over the phone in video chat, knowing it was something pertinent to the investigation into Roger's death. "An arrest has been made of the man we believe planted the surveillance devices at your uncle's house."

She perked up at the announcement. "How did you find him?"

"We were able to trace the serial numbers of some of the equipment back to the store where they were purchased—and ultimately to the person who bought the devices."

Her eyes widened. "Do you think he's the Violet Killer...?"

"That's yet to be determined," Dylan spoke frankly. "I'm about to interrogate him. We'll see how it goes." He practically expected her to ask if she could sit in on the interview, knowing the unsub had invaded not only Roger's privacy but Naomi's as well, not to mention may have been responsible for her uncle's death. But, at the moment, she seemed content to take a wait-and-see approach.

"I'll be waiting to hear what you find out," she told him equably.

"I'll let you know what happens," he spoke simply, and disconnected. For an instant, Dylan thought back to Naomi's cryptic words to her colleague Sophia he'd overheard from their phone call earlier. *I'll be careful.* By the look on Naomi's face, he'd gotten the distinct impression that she wasn't referring to the investigation into Roger's death. Or the serial killer case, in general. Dylan had a feeling it was more about being careful as it pertained to matters of the heart. As if to say she was fearful about moving into dangerous territory in rekindling their relationship. In fact, he would never hurt her willingly. Could she say the same about hurting him? Or was that the point—repeating history with the same result?

Casting these thoughts aside, Dylan gazed through the one-way glass into the interrogation room, where they had let the suspect sit by himself for a while, a common tactic in law enforcement designed to both frustrate and unnerve the person. His name was Tony Ketchum. The forty-four-year-old was an ex-employee of a security firm. He had been let go six months ago after being accused of illegally planting hidden cameras in a shopping mall women's restroom. Police investigated, but no charges were ever filed.

"What do you think?" Patricia asked, standing alongside Dylan in observing the chunky suspect with a slicked-back, salt-and-pepper-colored hairstyle. He was dressed in casual clothing. "Could this be our unsub?"

Hesitant to speculate on appearance alone, much less draw conclusions that may not pan out pending a thorough search of the suspect's residence and vehicle, Dylan answered coolly, "We're about to find out." Sure that the profiler was eager to take her own crack at the suspect, should this prove to be warranted, Dylan left her and Chief Frazier, with an equal interest in the outcome, to step into the room.

It was big enough to fit three or four people comfortably, but not so big as to waste space and make it less intimidating. There was a wooden rectangular table and two metal chairs. Dylan sat in the one unoccupied across from the suspect. He had been advised of his rights and gave no indication as yet of wanting a lawyer before speaking. Studying the man who at the very least was a voyeur and could well be a cunning serial killer, Dylan waited a beat before speaking. "I'm Detective Hester. Do you know why you're here, Mr. Ketchum…?"

The suspect, who was handcuffed, snorted. "They just told me it had to do with some illegal surveillance equipment. I thought this was already settled?"

"It was, if you're referring to the mall restroom investigation," Dylan said. "That's not why we're here."

Ketchum lowered thick brows over blue-gray eyes. "Then suppose you clue me in…"

"I'd be happy to." Dylan glanced at the one-way mirror. "Some hidden surveillance devices were found at the office and home of a private investigator named Roger Lincoln. Know anything about that?"

Ketchum reacted, clearly shaken. "Why would I?" he claimed.

"Because you were the one who planted them." Dylan peered at the suspect, fighting to maintain control at the prospect that he might have seen Naomi in the nude and enjoyed it. But he didn't believe that was necessarily the perp's primary objective.

"That's crazy," he insisted. "I don't know what you're talking about."

"Cut the crap, Ketchum." Dylan realized playing the nice guy was getting him nowhere. "We were able to trace the bugs back to you—including video surveillance of you purchasing them. There's DNA as well that I'm betting will link you even further to the crime. No sense in denying it, if you know what's good for you. Or not as bad as it's going to get. The bigger issue is what your motivation was for planting the devices. Care to tell me?"

Ketchum bottled up, as if weighing his options, which were few to none that could get him out of this trap. Dylan decided it was time to increase the pressure. "What do you know about the Violet Killer?"

The suspect cocked a brow ill at ease. "He's that serial killer, right?"

"Right." Dylan wondered if playing dumb was a halfhearted, last-ditch effort to save himself from a fate of his own making. "Besides strangling local women, the killer is also suspected of murdering Roger Lincoln. The same private eye whose house you bugged. Am I starting to connect the dots here easily enough for you to understand, Ketchum? Did you shoot to death Lincoln, who it just so happens was investigating the Violet Killer and about to close in on him?"

"Whoa!" Ketchum's voice shook. "I didn't kill anyone. And I'm not this Violet Killer."

"If you want to convince me of that, you'd best start talking—and fast!" Dylan regarded him with an intentional menacing look.

"Okay, okay," the suspect muttered, sighing.

"Yeah, I planted the bugs in Lincoln's house. But it had nothing to do with murder or a serial killer's vendetta…" Ketchum wrinkled his bulbous nose. "My ex-wife hired Lincoln to dig up dirt on me in a custody battle. I only planted the devices to learn what I could about what he knew, so I could be better equipped to fight her in court. That's it!"

Not entirely convinced, Dylan pressed him on some details they knew about the serial killer unsub and also Ketchum's whereabouts during the last three murders attributed to the Violet Killer. Ketchum seemed genuinely thrown by the questions and was able to account for his whereabouts during the days and times in question, subject to verification. "Would you be willing to take a lie detector test?" Dylan asked, using another name for a polygraph, which was routinely used by law enforcement agencies to try to rule in or out suspects in crimes. Though inadmissible in criminal court, it gave authorities a mostly reliable sense of whether the suspect was being truthful or not.

"Yeah, I'll take it," a rattled Ketchum agreed without preconditions.

Half an hour later, Gail Takamura, a forty-year-old licensed, professional polygraph examiner for the Pebble Creek PD and state of Oregon, administered the test. "The suspect passed it," she reported unceremoniously to Dylan, Patricia and Chief Frazier, after leaving the interrogation room. The thin, dark-haired examiner flashed amber eyes hotly. "He's not your Violet Killer."

Though disappointed, Dylan had already decided that Tony Ketchum was not their unsub. Aside from the polygraph results, honestly, he didn't see the out-of-shape former security firm worker as being athletic enough to chase down women as a serial killer and vanish quickly while leaving no evidence behind. Dylan was sure that the search of Ketchum's property would back him up.

Patricia was on the same page. "The real unsub would like nothing better than for us to nab someone like Ketchum to pay for his crimes, leaving him to possibly go elsewhere and pick up where the Violet Killer left off in Pebble Creek."

"So we're back to square one, more or less," Frazier grumbled.

"Not exactly," Dylan begged to differ. "We can eliminate at least one concern that the unsub had been spying on Naomi as an offshoot of his targeting of Roger. That said, Tony Ketchum is still guilty of planting surveillance devices illegally and will have to answer for that."

Everyone was in agreement. Unfortunately, this did little to ease Dylan's concern that the unsub was still a threat to Naomi and had to be taken seriously in this regard. As well as the danger posed to females throughout the town. Until they could put an end to his serial strangulation homicides and make the community safe again.

Chapter Thirteen

"The Violet Killer unsub wasn't the one responsible for planting the bugs in Roger's house and office," Dylan told Naomi as they stood in the great room.

Her eyes rolled with shock. "Seriously?"

"Wish I could say otherwise." He pursed his lips. "We would've loved to have been able to kill two birds with one stone, so to speak. But as it turns out, a man named Tony Ketchum put the devices in as part of a custody battle. His wife had hired Roger to investigate him and this was Ketchum's ill-advised attempt to gain the upper hand. In any event, he passed a polygraph and his alibis checked out for the latest Violet Killer murders." Dylan jutted his chin. "As such, he's been eliminated as a feasible unsub."

Naomi tried to hide her disappointment. The idea that the one who had spied on her uncle and was likely a voyeur on her movements around the house was a different creep altogether than the serial killer terrorizing the community was unsettling. To say the least. Moreover, it meant that the man who murdered her uncle Roger was still running free, snubbing his nose at all of them seeking his capture. "I suppose it was too much to expect that a homicidal perp who had successfully evaded the law for more than two years would trip himself up so easily," she moaned begrudgingly.

"Perhaps," Dylan agreed. He ran a hand through his thick hair. "All is not lost, though. The Violet Killer investigation is still ongoing, including ballistics assessments in trying to identify the gun used to kill Roger, and other leads we're pursuing. Even an effort to establish a link between shoeprints taken from the Sandra Neville crime scene and near the lake where you believe someone was watching you may yield some results in connecting dots."

Naomi nodded, feeling renewed sureness that the unsub would be brought to justice, one way or the other. "We'll get him," she spoke confidently. "In the meantime, it's good to know that the man who chose to invade my privacy has been apprehended."

"Yeah, there is that." Dylan's tone afforded the protective nature of their association she had come to expect and depend upon to a certain extent. "Thank goodness for not-so-small favors."

"Yes." She moved up to him as they stood by the rustic maple mantel. Sitting on it by its lonesome was the framed photograph of the two of them that her uncle had left to Dylan, almost as if for safekeeping. Naomi wasn't irked in the slightest that he had chosen not to give it to her, believing that the picture somehow belonged to Dylan as a reminder of everything that was once great about them. Something her uncle Roger was confident she would never lose sight of at the end of the day. Raising her eyes to Dylan's face, she asked impulsively, "Will you dance with me?"

Seemingly taken aback, he gave her an up-and-down look. "There's no music."

"Wait right here." Naomi dashed over to her cell phone she'd left on the coffee table. Grabbing it, she turned it on and went to her downloaded music, picked out a slow song and played it. Heading back over to Dylan, who hadn't budged from his spot, eyeing her with amusement, she challenged him. "Now what's your excuse?"

He gave her his trademark grin, putting his hands to her waist. "Can't think of one."

"Don't even try." She put her arms around his neck boldly. "Let's dance."

Dylan laughed. "It would be my pleasure."

They moved even closer together, bodies pressing and molding sensuously to configure to one another as they danced slowly, but surely. Naomi, drowning in his intoxicating manly scent, lost in Dylan's strong arms, felt that, indeed, the pleasure was all hers. Or at least as much as his, if not more. Being with him like this felt right. It would feel even better if she kissed him. Lifting her chin, she watched him lower his, clearly on the same wavelength, before their mouths met. And began to have a life of their own. Parting her lips ever so slightly, Naomi dived in for more smooching and tasting, prying Dylan's lips open to better accommodate her own. He acted accordingly, kissing her with the passion of two lovers, causing Naomi to feel as though she were floating on air. Held down only by his sturdy grip and hungry kiss.

Her senses heightened, breathing erratic and arousal off the charts, it was all she could muster to break free of the lip-lock. "Maybe we should pick this up in your bedroom."

Dylan gave her the benefit of his lustful but hesitant gaze. "You really think that's a good idea?"

Without trying to overthink things or, for that matter, underthink them, she responded desirously, "I can't think of a better one." She met his eyes daringly. "Can you...?"

He licked his lips as though ready to dive into a pan-fried T-bone steak. "Now that you mention it, I think it's an excellent idea. In fact, I believe you said something about picking this up... Think I'll get the ball rolling in that regard." Before Naomi could react, Dylan had hoisted her up and into his arms and started carrying her through the great room and up the stairs, where they would take an uncertain but needed journey down memory lane. Only with a very current approach to their sexual desires.

It was all Dylan could do not to jump Naomi's bones right on the spot when they were dancing and tasting each other's mouths. But he had shown some restraint, hard as it was, and managed to get them to the master suite. Though they had left the soulful music downstairs, he was quite confident that they would be able to make their own music, with all the notes humming lyrically.

Setting Naomi on her feet, Dylan began removing her clothes, eager to see her naked again. He had little doubt she would present the same picture of perfection that drove him nuts with wanton desire two years ago. As though eager to please, Naomi pitched in to hurriedly undress and display her nudity for his eyes only. She did not disappoint. All the curves and bends in the right package of taut slenderness. Her breasts were not too small, not too large, but just right—waiting to be caressed, the erect nipples tasted like sweet wine.

"You still like what you see?" Naomi's eyes widened teasingly.

"What's not to like?" Dylan licked his lips appetizingly. "You're a meal fit for a king."

"I'm happy to be your queen, Dylan." She gave him a toothy smile, while fumbling with the buttons on his shirt. "Do you have protection?"

"Yes." He was happy to see that, like him, she didn't confuse wanton desire with recklessness. If children were ever to become part of the picture for them, there would be a time and place for that. Right now, it was all about them and satisfying pent-up needs.

He removed his pants, underwear, shoes and socks, tossing them aside, till he was totally nude. His firm erection left little doubt where he stood in wanting to be with her. Naomi studied it in wonder while taking in the whole of his body. "You haven't changed a bit, I see," she gushed.

"Thanks, but I think I have," he corrected, and it had nothing to do with his workout regimen. Or healthy living to make for a healthy body. "You see, I'm two years wiser. And, as such, two years hungrier for a meal that only you can provide for the ultimate nourishment."

"I want you, too," she promised, a catch to her tone. "Like now!"

As she lay invitingly on the chenille bedspread, he got a condom out of the drawer of a weathered oak nightstand, tearing it open and swiftly putting it on. Without further delay, Dylan slid onto the bed and halfway into Naomi's waiting arms. There, they picked up where they left off, exchanging fiery kisses, moving from their mouths to cheeks and chins and back again to each other's lips. She was driving him crazy and he loved it. The need to be inside her building up like steam in a freight train, he nevertheless held back, wanting Naomi to need him even more than she did. Using the tips of his fingers, Dylan brought them down to her sweet spot and adroitly massaged till she was wet and wanting. She quivered mightily to his touch and left no doubt that he was succeeding in his endeavor.

"Make love to me, Dylan," begged Naomi. "I'm ready!"

"That's all I needed to hear," he told her in a deep tone of voice. Lifting up, Dylan sandwiched himself between her splayed legs. Entering her hot body, he drove in hard and often, with Naomi encouraging with each thrust. Her moans and movement were intoxicating to his libido, playing with his mind as well, with lust drowning out everything else. As she gripped his buttocks, he felt Naomi's powerful orgasm, her body shaking like an earthquake of satisfaction.

They had sex for as long as Dylan could stand it, before his need to explode took over. As his orgasm broke free, practically paralyzing him with the potent release, he sucked in a ragged breath and allowed nature to take its course. Naomi followed suit, as a second wave of climax manifested itself, allowing them to ride the wave of carnal delight in tandem, their slickened bodies moving harmoniously till reaching the end of the line.

Afterward, both lay still for a long moment, catching their breaths and sharing a few kisses for good luck, before uncoupling. "Was it as good for you as before?" Naomi asked, putting her mouth to his shoulder.

"I might have thought that was an impossible mountain to climb," Dylan said honestly, playing footsies with her. "But after what we just went through, I think it's obvious that the sex between us is better now than ever."

She blushed. "I can't argue with that."

"Neither can I." He touched one of her nipples, getting an immediate reaction. "Guess some things never die, but only strengthen with time." What that meant exactly in the scheme of their separate lives, Dylan wasn't sure. Were they meant to be only fantastic lovers but not soul mates? Why not both? Or was this laying the groundwork for some necessary give-and-take, especially on his part?

Naomi chuckled. "Maybe we're vampires that only needed to be reawakened," she quipped.

He laughed. "You can bite me anytime you like."

She nibbled playfully on his neck. "Don't give me any ideas."

Their easy banter and sheer sexual compatibility reminded Dylan of how good they were together. As if he could ever have forgotten. It was a welcome respite from working the Violet Killer case and stressing over it and keeping Naomi and other women out of harm's way. Suddenly, feeling reenergized, he found Naomi's mouth and conquered it again with hard kisses, for which she reciprocated in kind. He became aroused, as did she. One thing led to another, with him grabbing a condom, for a repeat performance. Only this time, having appeased their primordial urges, they were able to take it nice and slow. When it was finally over, Naomi rolled off Dylan and both started giggling like little children. But with decidedly adult sexual appetites.

As they lay there for a long, silent moment, Naomi propped on an elbow and asked pointedly, "So, where do you see this going...?" Her eyes sharpened at him. "Or was what just happened more about a roll in the hay for a fun trip down memory lane?"

Dylan cocked a brow in surprise. "Is that what you really think?" As Naomi mulled that over, considering it was she who initiated the sex, he couldn't resist throwing it back at her. "I could ask you the same thing."

Her mouth furrowed. "So why don't you?"

He knew why. Because Dylan didn't believe for one minute that all she wanted from him was to be taken to bed. Any more than merely sex, no matter how fantastic, was all he wanted from her. Indeed, he wanted so much more. The entire package. He just wasn't certain she felt the same way. At least as it pertained to living in the same place at the same time in pursuing a romance. "Long-distance relationships never work," he uttered pessimistically.

"That's because the parties involved fail to make a concerted effort to at least try to make it work," Naomi offered reasonably.

Dylan met her eyes. "Is that what you want, a long-distance relationship?" He noted that this had never been an option presented to him two years ago.

Thinking about the question, as though she had never zeroed in on it full-fledged till now, Naomi lowered her gaze and admitted waveringly, "I don't know…"

Just as they both contemplated their past and future, a cell phone rang. Dylan could tell from the peppy ringtone that it came from Naomi's phone. He actually welcomed the distraction to give them more time to assess what they wanted from each other and whether it was even possible to attain. "Better get that," he told her.

Unenthusiastically, Naomi rolled off the bed and Dylan enjoyed the view of her firm backside as she walked toward her clothes in a pile on the floor. Picking up cropped pants, she fished around for her cell phone before studying it. He watched her cringe, as though being the bearer of bad news. "What is it?" Dylan asked, sitting up.

"It's from him…" Her voice broke. Dylan climbed off the bed and met Naomi halfway. With a trembling hand, she held up the cell phone so he could read the text message with his own eyes:

Such a pretty violet. Too bad she had to die. You're next…

Dylan wrapped Naomi within his protective arms, fully understanding why she was shaken up. He cursed within at the thought that the unsub continued to harass her. To what end? Would he actually try to come after Naomi when they were ready and waiting for him to even try? Just as ominous was the implication that another young woman had been murdered by the Violet Killer. "Don't let this creep get to you," Dylan cautioned Naomi as best he could offer reassurance.

"How can I not?" she shot back. "I know it's just words. But they have meanings and since the unsub's already proven what he's capable of, I have to wonder when the frightening texts will turn into something more sinister."

As if on cue, Dylan's own cell phone rang. He reluctantly released Naomi from his grip and took a few steps to his floored trousers, lifting the phone from the back pocket. The caller was FBI Agent Patricia Stabler.

"Hey," he said tentatively. "What's up?"

"A woman was found dead this evening in her apartment." Patricia sucked in a deep breath. "Looks like the Violet Killer has struck again."

NAOMI ARRIVED AT the crime scene with Dylan. Though he would've preferred to spare her witnessing yet another murder, she believed it was incumbent upon her to see if the latest victim was another person of color. The fact that the unsub had chosen to make her part of his sick games made Naomi feel vulnerable. It also steeled her, making her more determined than ever to see him brought down. If she played any role in the woman's death, she needed to face it head-on and do her part to support the Task Force put together to halt the unsub in his tracks.

The three-story apartment complex was located on Camden Lane, not too far from Dylan's cabin, but far enough away that Naomi still felt safe there. In spite of the unsub's chilling texts and an unnerving sense that he was watching her every move, there was no solid proof that he had encroached upon Dylan's property. Much less, actually entered the cabin. Still, neither she nor Dylan were taking any chances, staying armed and ready, should the need arise to defend themselves.

Keeping up with Dylan as he worked his way through the usual barriers around and within the scene of a homicide, Naomi felt the loaded 9-millimeter Glock in a leather holster inside the waistband of her wide-leg slacks, worn with an oversize cardigan, reflecting a chill in the evening air. "I'm sure it's nothing you haven't seen before," Dylan advised her, "but be prepared anyway. Death is never a pretty sight."

"Tell me about it." Naomi rolled her eyes. Yes, apart from seeing enough of Sandra Neville's remains to stay with her, she had encountered corpses as a member of the Secret Service. Though unpleasant, it came with the territory. That included being thrown into the mix of a serial killer case. "I'll be fine," she assured him, even if still feeling a bit jittery after receiving the purported perp's text message.

"Okay." Dylan nodded before they approached Detective Hwang, Agent Stabler and other law enforcement personnel. Onlookers were being questioned and kept at bay. "What's the latest?" Dylan asked casually to no one in particular, having been filled in on some of the details before they arrived.

"The medical examiner has arrived to transport the body to the morgue," Hwang said. "Forensics is going through the apartment for evidence." He took a notepad out of his pocket and flipped through the pages. "The victim is a white female who has been identified by her roommate, Julia Bridges, as twenty-six-year-old Sylvie Maguire, a graduate student at Pebble Creek College and part-time bartender at the Owl Club on Bogue and Tenth Street. According to the roommate, when she got back home at approximately seven from class at Pebble Creek College, she found Maguire, fully clothed and lifeless on the floor in her bedroom. A violet was sticking out of her mouth."

Oddly, sad as it was to see another young woman lose her life, Naomi found some comfort in the fact that the latest murder did not appear to be race based. In spite of the texts that were clearly intended to intimidate her, as though it was personal. She chose to believe, as the profiler had indicated, the unsub's targets were less about physical characteristics and more about the often random nature of serial homicides and the opportunistic targeting, even when scoping out the victim's habits and locations prior to an attack.

Dylan cringed. "Is there a boyfriend or…?" Naomi immediately understood that Dylan was automatically going for the standard process of elimination. Female victims of homicide were much more likely to be murdered by current or ex intimates than any other type of offender. Exploiting a high-profile serial killer's MO by being a copycat murderer to throw the authorities off was not unheard of.

"She's been single for a while, says the roommate," Hwang responded, seemingly putting that angle to rest. "Still, we're checking her relationship status out, and also going door-to-door to assess the landscape and see if anyone saw anything."

"At least one person saw everything," Patricia said dreadfully, running a hand through her hair. "The perp who snuffed out the victim's life like a candle. With her fair skin and long, thick red locks, Sylvie Maguire could well have been my little sister. Instead, she has been denied the ability to carve out a long future with all its benefits."

Dylan bristled. "Yeah, it's probably the worst part of this for all the victims and their families."

Naomi felt the same, having experienced it first-hand with the loss of her uncle, whom she would never get to have long conversations with on the ups and downs of life. Not to mention, he would never have the opportunity to walk her down the aisle, assuming that were to ever happen. She considered briefly the amazing and all-consuming sex with Dylan earlier, reminding her of just how good things were between them before she left two years ago. Now they seemed to be at a crossroads in determining where they went in their relationship. Would she call making love one time—make that twice—as intense and unforgettable as it was, a relationship? Would he? Was there enough there to bridge the gap that still seemed as wide as Pebble Creek Lake itself?

"I understand you received another text message, Naomi," Patricia said, breaking through her reverie.

Snapping out of it, Naomi saw that Dylan and Hwang were now bringing Chief Frazier up to speed. "Yes," she told the profiler. "It came just before we learned about the latest victim." Naomi warmed at the thought of making love to Dylan mere minutes before they were brought back to reality in stark and distressed fashion.

"Can I see it?"

"Sure." Naomi took out her cell phone and brought up the text, which still left her on edge.

Such a pretty violet. Too bad she had to die. You're next...

"Hmm..." Patricia frowned. "So, he's continuing to harass you, even while murdering others..."

"I think he may be stalking me in person, as well." Naomi squirmed as she thought about the man watching her in the lake.

Patricia acknowledged as much. "Dylan mentioned it."

"What do you suppose it means, if anything?" Naomi questioned, ill at ease. "Is it a warning of more intimidation to come? Or does the perp have something much worse in his demented mind where it concerns me?" She shuddered to think of what he could be planning, if orchestrated successfully.

"Let me work on that in the unsub's psychological profile," Patricia responded willingly. "Could be that I'm missing something here. If so, I'll find it. In the meantime, I suggest you not let your guard down, for even a minute. The worst thing you could do would be to underestimate the threat, which could only embolden the person who's doing this into further, more decisive actions."

"I get the picture." Naomi felt her firearm and wondered if she would be called upon to use it to defend herself. "I'll keep my eyes open." She knew Dylan would as well, along with the extra patrols he had ordered for the neighborhood. Perhaps that would be enough to do the trick. Either that or give the unsub greater determination to succeed in what he had in mind.

Naomi turned as the medical examiner came out, identified by Patricia. Dr. Martha Donahue looked tired, but made a beeline for Chief Frazier and Dylan. "The victim was definitely strangled to death," she told them dolefully. "As to a more definitive analysis, I should have the completed autopsy report in the morning."

After she answered a couple of routine questions, the body bag containing the corpse of Sylvie Maguire, the Violet Killer's newest victim, was carted away.

Chapter Fourteen

The next day, Dylan headed to the medical examiner's office to get the official word on Sylvie Maguire's death. Though this was more or less routine, it was never as simple as that to him. Each victim who died at the hands of the unsub was a human being—or had been prior to her murder—and deserved to be respected in that regard and given a decent burial. Knowing precisely how they died and connecting it with a single perpetrator would keep the focus on apprehending the killer and giving the victims the ability to rest in peace, accordingly. More than that, Dylan wanted to do his best to keep Naomi from a similar fate. With the unsub feeling brazen enough to send her frightening text messages and possibly stalking her, Dylan would move heaven and earth to protect Naomi. Whether they were on the path toward a reawakening of their romance or had mind-blowing sex to release pent-up passions with no expectations for more remained to be seen. Neither of them had talked about it after getting back to the cabin last night—each retreating to their separate bedrooms to sleep alone—as if to do so would only lead to more harm than good. For his part, Dylan knew he wanted Naomi for much more than a one-night stand. He sensed she felt the same. So why was it so hard for them to own up to this and do something about it? Would they really allow themselves to miss the mark again, knowing that second chances rarely turned into third ones?

Arriving at his destination, Dylan let the thoughts rest for now, as he refocused on his detective side and a serial killer case that continued to dog him and the Pebble Creek PD. And would not let up for them and the Task Force, till they could wrap up the investigation. This wouldn't happen unless the unsub was brought to his knees.

Martha Donahue was all business upon his arrival to her spacious office with a nice view out of a square pivot window. "Since I have a couple more autopsies to perform and we're both pretty busy these days," she said, "I'll cut to the chase, Detective Hester. Sit." She proffered him a black task chair in front of the desk, where she was seated.

He sat down, leaning back. "How did she die?" he asked with anticipation.

Martha touched her glasses, then glanced at the monitor on her desk. "Ms. Maguire's official cause of death was due to asphyxiation, as a result of ligature strangulation. I estimate that the time of death was anywhere from around five to seven yesterday evening."

Dylan's brows knitted. He imagined how torturous it had to have been to be suffocated to death. "You think it was the same killer as the other women?" he asked straightforwardly, for the record.

Martha wrinkled her nose. "As I always like to point out, I'm a medical examiner, not a detective, Dylan. That being said, having followed the Violet Killer case closely, based on the autopsies done on the victims, the similarities are too striking to believe they were committed by different individuals. Right down to the violet left behind that never varies in size, shape and color. So, there you have it, Detective, in a nutshell."

Dylan nodded, having already reached the same conclusion in looking at the signs pointing entirely in one direction. "Any indication of sexual assault?" He had to ask, even if the victim was fully dressed when discovered. Or that it went against the grain of the unsub's modus operandi. But MOs could change. And it also wouldn't be the first time a perp had forced sex upon a victim with her clothes on.

"There's no evidence that the decedent was sexually assaulted," the medical examiner stated. "Nor, for that matter, was there evidence that the victim had engaged in consensual sex on the day she died."

"Just checking, for the record."

"Understood." Martha sat back. "Any more questions?"

"That's it for now." Dylan rose, pushing aside the possibility that someone other than their unsub was responsible for Sylvie Maguire's murder. That meant they could officially, more or less, make her female victim number nine of the Violet Killer, with Roger, a male casualty, increasing the total to at least ten known victims to date.

WHEN NAOMI GOT a call from Patricia Stabler asking her to come into the police department for a chat, she readily agreed, anxious to see what the profiler had come up with in trying to get into the unsub's head. Just as he was trying to get into Naomi's own head, and succeeding, to some degree. On the whole, though, she refused to buckle under to his lunatic tricks, knowing this would give him all the power in a tug-of-war she had to win. For herself, the other women targeted and her uncle.

Naomi saw Patricia seated at a desk in the back of a rather large room with cubicles for the various detectives and FBI agents. Most were empty at the moment, as nearly all hands were on deck in the Violet Killer investigation. She passed by a metal desk that used to belong to her Uncle Roger but, seeing the nameplate, was now occupied by Dylan. Naomi had mixed feelings. She was certainly happy for Dylan that he had rightfully been promoted to his current position and held it with pride. But she felt saddened at the thought that her uncle had retired too soon, which, through no fault of his own other than doing his new job in private investigation, paved the way for someone to take his life.

"Good morning," Patricia said cheerfully, having stood up to greet her.

"Good morning," Naomi returned and ran a hand through her hair.

"Welcome to my little neck of the woods. With any good fortune, it'll be short-lived and I can go wherever they tell me to next—"

"It's a tough life." Naomi admittedly could relate. Working for the Secret Service, she had often traveled far and wide from home, leaving little time for a social life. Was she really okay with that? Or had spending time with Dylan given her cause to reassess what her priorities in life should be? And what they should not be.

"It can be," Patricia spoke musingly. "It can certainly wreak havoc on one's love life." She took a breath. "But hey, we all make choices, professionally and personally, and have to live with the consequences, for better or worse."

"True," Naomi agreed, but didn't necessarily feel good about it for the FBI agent or herself. Maybe they both needed to make some better choices in their lives. Or possibly end up alone and wondering what went wrong to put them there.

"Have a seat," Patricia said, sitting back at the desk.

Naomi took the faux leather side chair and adjusted herself.

Patricia clasped her hands. "Based on what you've been going through with the text messages and apparent stalking by presumably the same person believed to be responsible for the Violet Killer murders, I've reworked my psychological profile of the unsub, as it relates to you."

"Tell me…" Naomi leaned forward, hanging on the profiler's every word with more than a little interest.

"All right." Patricia took a breath. "Having evaluated the texts and the killer's overall tendencies as a serial stalker and murderer, I believe that his infatuation with you goes well beyond the fact that you and he are indirectly connected through Roger. My sense is that the unsub may have come into contact with you directly in some way."

Naomi's eyes widened with shock. "You mean face-to-face?"

"Not necessarily, but it is certainly a possibility."

"When? Where? Are we talking about since I've returned to Pebble Creek?" The notion unnerved her.

Patricia stiffened. "Perhaps. But more likely, you and he may have met or known each other even before your return," she suggested. "The unsub could have discovered this inadvertently when stealing your uncle's laptop, thereby triggering in the recognition an unnatural fascination, which the unsub may have seen as somehow meant to be in his warped state of mind."

"Are you saying the Violet Killer could be someone I knew at any time in my life?" Naomi's lower lip hung down. "Like from high school? College? Even before then? What?"

"More likely, it's much more recent than that," Patricia said coolly. "You could have met him while shopping, socializing, exercising or through some other means. Could be that it was only in passing or happenstance, possibly without your even being aware of it. But through his eyes, it is a connection that he cannot resist acknowledging in his own way through the text messages and stalking from a safe distance. If this is the case, that will likely escalate into attempting to reach you in a face-to-face way, to fulfill whatever fantasies he may have conjured up during the progression."

Naomi felt sick as she digested all that had been said. The thought that this psychopath could have been within feet of her before he began killing women was unsettling, to say the least. What if he had gone after her before she left Pebble Creek—ending her career with the Secret Service before it began? Then she would never have been given the opportunity to work her way back to Dylan, no matter what the future may hold for them. "How does this supposed scenario factor into the unsub's serial killer cravings?" she dreaded to ask. "Or are the two somehow unrelated in his damaged mind?"

"Oh, they are definitely related," the profiler responded. "I believe the unsub suffers from some level of attachment disorder. In needling you through the texts and stalking, he sees it as merely a means to the same ending he had inflicted upon the other victims of his obsession—death."

Naomi mused uncomfortably. "Could I have somehow encouraged this lunatic without realizing it?" She hated to think that he had become obsessed through her own unintended actions.

"I seriously doubt that." Patricia jutted her chin.

"This has nothing to do with your behavior and everything to do with his."

"Is there any way to get him to lay off?" Naomi asked with desperation. "Such as telling the perp I'm not interested in a reply text? Or would that only embolden him and freak me out even more?"

"You definitely do not want to provoke him by contacting him in any form," stressed Patricia. "I'm only telling you this for informational purposes to better understand what we're dealing with here as it relates to what you're experiencing. I intend to run this by the team, but wanted to talk to you first. Let us do the heavy lifting in pursuing and stopping the unsub."

"I will," Naomi promised, knowing deep down inside that playing with fire could only get her burned. She wasn't going to go Lone Ranger in pursuing her stalker outside the investigators, including Dylan, tasked with bringing him down. "Sorry I asked."

"Nothing to apologize for, Naomi." Patricia reached out and touched her hand. "This has all of us a little freaked out. We're on top of it and beyond till the end."

Naomi nodded and gave a comforted smile. She appreciated being given a new perspective in characterizing the unsub, even if it left her wondering who it might be. And if there was any way to jar her memory in producing an image the Task Force could work with in identifying the killer.

"WE'VE GOT A hit on the gun used to shoot Roger," Hwang told Dylan as they walked and talked on the first floor of the police department. "Or not so much the actual weapon, but important info about the firearm."

"Go on..." Dylan pressed, taking anything they could get in advancing their objectives in this case.

"According to the National Integrated Ballistic Information Network, based on data entered into the system on the bullet that killed Roger and the ballistic markings on the shell casing, they were able to link it to bullets that came from the same weapon that has a gun barrel with a left-hand twist and four lands and grooves. The .45 ACP handgun was used earlier this year in an armed robbery at a party store in nearby Stafford Heights that left one man dead and a woman critically injured. The robber-shooter, identified as forty-seven-year-old Aidan Powell, was killed three weeks later when his car spun out of control on Route 18. The murder weapon was never found."

"Hmm..." Dylan mused aloud. "So, someone else—the unsub—ended up with this same firearm and used it on Roger?"

Hwang nodded. "My guess is that Powell dumped the murder weapon into the black market and the unsub snatched it up, not wanting to use a registered gun to do his dirty work."

"Makes sense in a homicidal perp's way of thinking," conceded Dylan, feeling frustrated that the killer seemed to somehow continue to stay a step or two ahead of them. But that calculating could go only so far before he could no longer press his luck and come out ahead. "We need to find that gun—and the triggerman himself," Dylan declared. "I think there's no doubt that if strangling his victims won't do the trick or he's otherwise backed into a corner, the unsub's more than willing to shoot anyone who gets in his way."

"Yeah, that's the scary part," Hwang muttered. "Not that the citizens of Pebble Creek could be any more frightened these days, so long as the Violet Killer remains at large. On that front, I've got some more news you need to hear."

"What is it?" Dylan stopped midway as they scaled the stairs for the second floor, where their desks were located. He gazed at Hwang's unreadable eyes.

"Forensics matched the size-ten shoeprint found near Sandra Neville's remains with the footprint you located at the spot by the lake near your cabin," the detective told him.

"Really?" Dylan's voice rose. "Are they sure about that?"

"They're pretty confident that the prints are the same size, same manufacturer, same impressions left on the grass. Could be entirely coincidental or circumstantial evidence that the same man was wearing the shoes at both scenes—your call…" Hwang started moving up the steps again with Dylan. "If you ask me, I think Naomi is on to something that our unsub has been tracking her, while at the same time going after other women. Unless we stop him, it's only a matter of time before she becomes his main focus—"

"Yes, that's what I'm afraid of," Dylan said worriedly, sensing all along that the unsub had some kind of fixation on Naomi and could try to raise the stakes at any time. He wasn't about to let that happen. Not so long as Dylan was still breathing. Once they reached the second floor, he told Hwang, "For the record, I don't believe in coincidences any more than you do." That included the dark SUV that Naomi believed was following her, which they had yet to track down.

Hwang gave a half smile and patted him on the shoulder. "Never thought for a moment that you did."

Dylan acknowledged this and headed toward his desk, when he spotted Patricia and Naomi moving toward him. Both had serious looks on their faces and he felt a twinge in the pit of his stomach in wondering what was on their minds.

"Ladies," he said in a gentlemanly tone, belying his curiosity. "What's up?"

"We've got a new angle on the unsub…" Naomi spoke ambiguously. He saw the unease in her eyes, almost as though she were about to cry. But she blinked this away and extended her chin resistantly.

"I believe the Violet Killer's fixation on Naomi may go deeper than we ever thought." Patricia batted her lashes. "Let's assemble the Task Force now and talk about it."

"TAKE A GOOD look at the suspects' faces," Dylan told Naomi, as she strode up to the bulletin board and studied the large photographs. Patricia had laid out to the Task Force her revised criminal profile on the unsub, with the belief that his fixation on Naomi, in particular, was most likely developed from a past connection, real or imagined. And that it would probably progress to a deadly obsession, if allowed to go unchecked. As she grappled with this terrifying prospect, Dylan and Hwang had shown a correlation between footprints found at the scene of Sandra Neville's dead body and the area where Naomi believed a man had been checking her out through binoculars. The detectives also pointed out the fatal path of the gun used to kill her uncle Roger. All of which sent a chill up and down Naomi's spine. She examined each photograph carefully, knowing she would be given all the time she needed, especially if she were able to positively identify someone she recognized. But she drew a blank. None of the men—some more intriguing than others in facial structure, hairstyle or eye color—particularly stood out as someone who looked familiar. Was that because she simply couldn't remember? Or had never pinned it down to memory? Naomi sucked in a deep breath. The more likely answer, as Patricia had suggested, was that the connection, if one could call it that, was one-sided. It was all in the head of a psychopath. Making him all the more disturbing and dangerous.

She turned away from the bulletin board and gazed right into the intense gray eyes of Dylan. "I'm sorry," she uttered sincerely, "but I don't recognize any of these men."

Instead of expressing disappointment, he seemed

to take it in stride. "Not a problem. The unsub is most likely someone you have no knowledge of, while concealed in open view. It was worth a shot." The hard lines in Dylan's face softened. "Don't worry, I won't let him get anywhere near you."

"I know." Naomi didn't doubt for one second his commitment to her as the lead detective on the case. She wasn't as certain about his commitment to her as a man and lover. Or vice versa. That was something they would have to address at a later time. When they weren't in a room full of law enforcement personnel whose sole mission was to capture a serial murderer before anyone else could be strangled or shot to death. "If the unsub should try," she spoke bravely, "I'll do whatever I need to protect myself. Or anyone he might go after."

Dylan's eyes crinkled satisfyingly. "Wouldn't expect anything less from you, Secret Service Agent Lincoln."

Naomi offered him a smile and took a seat in the front, while Chief Frazier took to the podium and gave what amounted to a pep talk in encouraging the Task Force members not to let up even in the slightest, till they had the Violet Killer in custody. Or he was taken out of commission, should it come to that. No one went against the grain in their shared determination to see this endeavor through successfully.

Chapter Fifteen

Later that afternoon, Naomi invited Brenda Quinlan, the woman her uncle Roger had been seeing before his death, for tea. She had gotten Brenda's number from his cell phone, feeling compelled to make contact with someone he had obviously cared for. Also, Naomi had hoped her uncle might have said something to her, even inadvertently, that could provide a clue about the killer. Dylan's cabin seemed the safest place to meet in protecting herself, with no reason to believe the unsub would go after the woman her uncle had been romantically involved with and was otherwise no threat to him.

"Thanks for reaching out to me," Brenda said with a smile, wearing a cream-colored, wide-brimmed floppy hat as they sat on the Adirondack chairs on the deck.

"Thanks for coming." Naomi smiled back and lifted her teacup, filled with chai tea. "Since you were in my uncle's life toward the end of it, I thought it might be nice to talk."

"I agree. Roger would've loved for us to get to

know one another. He couldn't wait for you to return home to put that into motion."

"I wish I had come before it was too late," Naomi expressed, sensing the sadness and regret from her, which she too felt. "But life always seemed to get in the way, whether an adequate excuse or not." Knowing her uncle, Naomi was sure he would be admonishing her for going down that road, as one who always believed that she was doing what she was supposed to and he encouraged such to the very end of his life.

"That's normal," Brenda said, sipping her tea. "Roger knew that and couldn't have been prouder of you."

Naomi blushed. "I felt the same about him."

"The man was never dull and definitely a good catch." Brenda showed her teeth. "We had plans to go to the jazz festival in Seattle next year."

"I know he would have enjoyed that," Naomi said, remembering his appreciation for such great jazz vocalists as Ella Fitzgerald and Sarah Vaughan. It just wasn't meant to be. Or, if it was, the unsub had disrupted any such plans. On that thought, Naomi gazed at Brenda and, after tasting the tea, asked causally, "Did my uncle happen to mention anything to you about any of the cases he was working on?"

Thinking about the question for a moment or two, she responded, "Not that I can recall. He didn't seem all that interested in talking much about his work, focusing mostly on light subjects, hobbies and getting what he could out of life." Brenda eyed her curiously. "I've been keeping track of the murder investigation. Are you working now with the police in the investigation?"

"Yes, I'm offering consultation, as a witness to the crime," admitted Naomi, hoping this might spur something in her. "My uncle's laptop and all his files were taken by his killer. The laptop's been found and we're trying to retrieve any pertinent info from it, but that could take a while. I just thought that maybe Uncle Roger, talkative as he could be, might have confided in you anything that could be helpful in the investigation."

Brenda tasted more tea thoughtfully. "Come to think of it, the last time I spoke with him, Roger did mention something about finally finding the missing pieces of a mystery that he couldn't shake. He didn't elaborate on it, but seemed confident that it was something he was about to solve."

"Only he never got the chance to," Naomi said, wrinkling her nose, wondering what those missing pieces were that might lead them to his killer.

"Maybe he did solve it," suggested Brenda. "I know he spent a lot of time on his laptop, sometimes even when we were together. If you're ever able to get those missing files, you could have the answer you're looking for."

Naomi believed that to be true, as well. But could Sophia recover what the unsub had intentionally destroyed? And, if so, would it come too late to save more lives at the hands of the serial killer?

"GOOD IDEA TO speak with Brenda," Dylan told Naomi, as they ate the Italian sausage lasagna she made that evening, along with red kale and sweet corn bread. Not used to cooking for anyone other than herself these days, Naomi liked the idea of making meals for Dylan. Didn't they say that good food was the way to a man's heart? Or would it take more than that to win him over again in full? "I believe that those missing pieces of a mystery are within our reach, one way or the other."

"Hope so." She forked a slice of lasagna, gazing at him. "That time can't come soon enough, with a creepy, unstable unsub seemingly lurking around every corner just waiting to strike when we least expect it."

"But that's perhaps his Achilles' heel," Dylan said sharply. "We are expecting him to make a move toward you—at least it seems like that's part of his illogical thought process. If that's the case, we'll be ready."

Naomi's lashes batted at him. "You mean use me to set a trap?"

"Not a chance!" Dylan's voice snapped. "I would never put your life on the line as bait, trust me." He wiped his mouth with a napkin. "What I meant was after what Patricia laid out, we won't take any chances that the unsub might try to up the ante. Until we get him, I've got an officer outside 24/7 and regular patrols that should deter even the most determined foe, when I'm not around myself."

"I see." Admittedly, she was content to have him

so concerned for her welfare, in spite of the fact that Naomi had grown used to protecting herself. But she had never dealt with someone so diabolical and unbalanced as the Violet Killer. While he might not pursue her back to Miami, as long as she remained in Pebble Creek, he posed a clear and present danger. Dylan understood that and had her back. She wouldn't have wanted it any other way. Except perhaps if what he felt was more romantic affection than he'd let on.

"Glad you do," Dylan said easily, eating more food. "Whatever else may have ended things between us before, we're in this together."

Naomi smiled, feeling reassured, maybe in more ways than one. "Yes, I believe we are."

That night, they slept in the same bed. Rather than try to psychoanalyze each other's intentions or overthink things as far as the future was concerned, they mutually agreed to put such thoughts aside, as well as the ins and outs of the Violet Killer investigation, in favor of the powerful sexual chemistry between them here and now. Naomi excitedly gave in to desire, feeding off Dylan's erotic cravings, as they made love well into the wee hours of the morning. Each gave as much as they took in the battle for physical appeasement, reaching time and time again, till spent.

Before she fell asleep, her head comfy on Dylan's hard chest, Naomi knew what her rapidly beating heart was telling her in no uncertain terms. She was still very much in love with Dylan. Whether he wanted to hear this or not or if it would make any difference in how they moved forward was still very much in question.

THE NEXT MORNING, Dylan slipped from bed, with Naomi still sound asleep like an angel. He could watch her beautiful face at peace all day, if only there weren't more pressing concerns to deal with. Namely, catching a serial killer. One who would like nothing better than to add Naomi to his list of deadly conquests, if given the opportunity. Dylan watched her for a bit longer, feeling aroused at the thought of the incredible sex that once again took his breath away last night, leaving him wanting more and more of her sexy body and gentle soul. Not to mention her intelligence, humor and drive, all presenting the complete picture of perfection as a remarkable woman. What was there not to love? When had he ever stopped loving her, whether he tried to convince himself otherwise? It was what to do with this love that threw Dylan for a loop. Was there still a chance they could have a go at a relationship? He still wanted it all from her. But was he willing to do whatever it took to make that happen in a way that was equally agreeable to Naomi?

Dylan chewed on those thoughts as he got dressed, had a quick bite to eat and headed off to work. He checked in with the officer on duty named Ed Palmer, a US Navy veteran, age thirty-three, who sat alert in his vehicle, before Dylan got into his own car. He started the ignition and drove away from his property with Naomi still occupying the better part of his mind.

No SOONER HAD he pulled onto the highway, when Dylan's cell phone rang. He was surprised to see that the caller was his sister, Stefany Gonzalez. His first thought was that there was something wrong. Though they were close—or as close as siblings could be who lived on different continents—busy lives kept them from having frequent contact. Okay, he admitted to himself that was a lame excuse for not communicating regularly in today's times of cell phones, the internet and social media.

Dylan accepted the video chat as he glanced at the phone in the dashboard mount. "Hey, sis."

Stefany's beautiful oval face appeared on the screen. It was surrounded by sun-drenched, short flaxen hair in an asymmetric style. "Hey, little brother." Her bluish-green eyes, inherited from their mother, twinkled. "I had a little time to kill and thought I'd check in on you to see how you're doing."

"Good to hear from you, Stefany." He grinned, noting she was wearing her medical scrubs, working with Doctors Without Borders in Southern Africa. "How's Theodore?"

"Busy like me, trying to keep up with our patients and their many needs."

"If anyone can do it, you can," Dylan stressed, proud of her for her dedication to the job and marriage at the same time. He wanted to experience that combo, too, but needed the right partner to complete his life. She was within reach, yet still just outside his grasp. Or so it seemed.

"I do my best." Stefany chuckled and then turned serious. "So, what's going on in your world?"

"Same old, same old," he said, wanting to spare her the mundane and uncomfortable aspects of his daily life.

She frowned. "I heard that you're still dealing with a serial killer run amok there."

Dylan winced. "Yeah, it's been an aggravating problem we're working overtime to solve," he groaned.

"And you will, Dylan," she encouraged him. "Stopping bad guys is what you were meant to do."

"Sometimes I wonder about that," he admitted, feeling the burden of the profession in dealing with a persistent unsub who didn't know when to quit. Dylan watched the road, then glanced back at her.

Stefany pursed her lips. "I can't imagine you doing anything else."

He felt the same way, as he loved police work; but Dylan couldn't help but wonder if he might be better suited to a new line of work. One in which stress and strain were less of an issue. And he had more time to do the things he truly loved like boating and, more than that, being in a committed relationship, where he could spoil the love of his life with affection, attention and anything else she wanted. Was it time for a change? Could he make it happen? Dylan looked at his sister. "I do have news."

"What?" Stefany asked anxiously.

"You'll never guess who's back in town."

"In that case, just tell me," she insisted.

"Naomi." Dylan waited for a reaction. He knew that Stefany had accused him of letting her get away, placing the blame for their relationship coming to a screeching halt squarely on his shoulders. For a while, he had resented the charge, believing he had done the right thing by allowing Naomi to chart her own course without his interference in putting undue pressure on her. Now he agreed with his sister and took full ownership of blowing his chance with Naomi. Had he asked her to marry him two years ago, it would have at the very least put everything on the table, for better or worse.

Shock registered across Stefany's face. "Oh, really?"

"Yeah. Naomi's uncle, Roger Lincoln, was killed and she came for the funeral."

"So sorry to hear about that," Stefany expressed.

"Yeah, it hit her hard." Dylan glanced at the small screen. "Now she's part of the Violet Killer Task Force." He explained the connection between Roger and the unsub, including Naomi witnessing her uncle's execution.

"Wow." Stefany's voice dropped a sorrowful octave. "I can't imagine what Naomi must be going through."

"She's dealing with it," Dylan spoke levelly, nearing his destination.

"And how are you dealing with seeing Naomi again?" Stefany put out bluntly. "Or shouldn't I ask?"

"She's staying with me," he said tonelessly, "for safety purposes." At least it started out that way. He thought about how far they had come in such a short time. "We're working through our issues."

Stefany smoothed a thin eyebrow. "Are you saying you might get back together?"

Dylan considered that the sex between him and Naomi was hotter than ever, proving that the sexual chemistry had never disappeared. And they seemed just as compatible intellectually. Even on a professional level, they had no problem being in sync. To him, this was an opening he was determined not to let close again. If he had any real say in it. But he thought it best not to get his sister's hopes—or even his own—up. Just in case his best efforts to keep Naomi in his life proved all for naught. "Let's just say anything's possible," he responded, leaving it at that.

Stefany seemed content with the response and didn't pry further. "Well, I have patients to get back to, so…"

"So, I'll let you go," Dylan said smilingly, reaching the police department. "Talk to you soon, sis." He meant it this time, recognizing that they needed each other, even from a great distance. Just as he needed Naomi, with the distance part yet to be determined.

"You better." Stefany peered at him and gave a little wave before hanging up.

Dylan parked in his spot. He grinned when thinking about his wise big sister. The notion of her and Naomi being sisters-in-law appealed to him. He imagined they could learn a lot from each other.

But he still needed to put a ring on Naomi's finger. Would she accept it as his future wife two years after he failed to propose the first time around? Or could he be setting himself up for another big disappointment?

Before he could go there, Dylan knew they had to deal with the Violet Killer, once and for all. If Patricia's assessment of the unsub was accurate, then Naomi was at even greater risk of his psychopathic obsession. Making it all the more imperative that they nail the perp without delay.

Dylan exited the car and headed toward the building.

Chapter Sixteen

"I think we have something…" forensic print analyst Vince Iverson told Dylan, Chief Frazier, Hwang and other law enforcement members of the Task Force in the conference room.

"Go on," Dylan urged him, noting the enthusiasm in his voice.

"All right." Iverson scratched his flat top. "From the latest identified victim of the Violet Killer, Sylvie Maguire, we were able to pull a latent palm print from a tennis bracelet she was wearing when killed. We ran it through the FBI's Next Generation Identification biometrics and criminal history system of digital and automated information and got a hit." He took a breath and turned to the bulletin board. "The print matched one on file for a DWI for Zachary Jamieson."

"The florist worker?" Dylan said, as the name registered immediately. The thirty-five-year-old was one of their primary suspects as the Violet Killer. The fact that Jamieson had a predilection for violets, in particular, and had been caught hanging around the crime scene where schoolteacher Conchita

Kaplan's body was discovered made him an obvious early suspect. But they had not been able to make anything stick. Till now.

"Yeah," Iverson confirmed, "it's him."

"I want Jamieson picked up immediately," Frazier ordered. "If this is our unsub, we don't want to give him an opportunity to escape our dragnet."

"We're on it!" Hwang declared.

"While we're all on the same page here," Dylan said, "we need to get a search warrant ASAP for Jamieson's residence and vehicle for evidence of his criminality. That includes the firearm used to kill Roger Lincoln. The unsub may have also chosen to hang on to Roger's own handgun, as a keepsake, which would be further evidence tying the serial murderer to Roger's death."

Frazier's brows twitched. "Get a judge to sign the order and let's get the evidence we need to put this guy away and take back our community!"

Dylan felt his blood pressure rise with the possibility that they could be one step closer to ending this nightmare in Pebble Creek. But before he told Naomi the news, only to give her false hope, Dylan wanted more concrete evidence that they had their unsub and he wasn't getting away to hurt her or any other woman ever again.

THE OLD FOURSQUARE stucco house was located on Ashford Street at the end of the tree-lined block. Dylan, Hwang and Agent Stabler, along with other police and FBI agents, approached the last known residence of Zachary Jamieson cautiously and with guns drawn, along with a search warrant. Though there was no sign of the red Jeep Renegade registered to Jamieson, Dylan went with the assumption that the suspect may still be inside the house, armed and very dangerous. The plan was to take him in alive, if at all possible. It was the only way to delve into the mindset of a purported serial killer for future reference. But that would be up to Jamieson, should it come to that.

Once they had ascended the house's porch steps, Dylan directed others to take their positions and be ready for whatever went down. He then gave the door a hard knock and yelled, "This is the police. Open up!" When there was no response, Dylan repeated the order sharply. Again, nothing from inside. Fearful that the suspect might try something dangerous, Dylan eyed two burly officers and nodded permission to break open the front door. They used a metal ram for the door breaching, bursting through.

With a Smith & Wesson M&P40 pistol in hand, Dylan led the others inside the two-and-a-half story residence. The first thing he noticed was the flowery-sweet scent of violets. Patricia noted it, too. "You can tell he's a florist," she quipped humorlessly, while holding her .38 Special revolver straight up.

Dylan sneered, eyes darting left and right for any signs of movement and seeing none. "That's not the half of it."

"Tell me about it," she agreed, as they walked across the mosaic-tiled entryway and onto the engineered hardwood floor.

Traditional furnishings were accented with vases filled with violets. The welcoming facade aside, as if leading the unsuspecting down a dark hole, Dylan signaled for the investigators to fan out. He took the lead in heading up the straight staircase to the second floor. After going from room to room, it was clear that no one was present. It appeared as though someone had left in a hurry. Could Jamieson have somehow been tipped off?

Once he was able to lower his guard, Dylan put the firearm back in his shoulder holster. The team's mission for the moment turned to a search for hard evidence. Donning nitrile gloves, he started with the master bedroom, digging through drawers and looking under the bed. Nothing of note, beyond a plastic bag of what appeared to be crystal methamphetamine. Dylan ignored the illicit drug possession for the time being, as he turned to the closet. Rifling through clothes and pushing aside shoes, he spotted a box on the shelf. Removing it, he looked inside and saw what Dylan was certain was a .45 ACP pistol. Much like the one used to take out Roger.

"What do we have here?" Patricia's eyes grew when Dylan held up the weapon downstairs.

"Is that what I think it is?" Hwang asked attentively.

"One can only hope." Dylan flashed them a deadpan look, not willing to get ahead of himself till ballistics was able to confirm that this was indeed the Roger Lincoln murder weapon.

An hour later, the verdict was in. At the crime lab,

George Suina was practically giddy and subdued at the same time, when he announced, "The .45 ACP handgun you discovered was the one used to shoot to death Roger Lincoln."

"Are you sure?" Dylan asked, more for effect than anything. He knew that the firearms and forensic investigator wasn't one for putting out speculation over facts. Especially when it came to solving a homicide as part of a broader investigation into a serial murderer. But it didn't hurt to hear him say it again as it related to this case.

"As sure as we're standing here," Suina declared, turning from Dylan to Hwang to Patricia, and back again at his workstation. He turned to his monitor, which showed a split screen. "We test-fired a bullet still in the chamber of the .45 ACP firearm from a gun barrel with four lands and grooves with a left-hand twist and matched it to the bullet used to shoot Roger. The ballistic markings on the shell casings were identical—meaning they could only have come from the same weapon."

"The murder weapon," Patricia said with an edge to her husky voice.

"When we couple that with the fingerprint linking Zachary Jamieson to Sylvie Maguire's murder, looks like we've finally put the solid pieces together to nail Roger's murderer and the Violet Killer," Hwang stated with satisfaction.

Dylan nodded, feeling uplifted that they knew who the unsub was. "Now we just need to locate Jamieson before he can hurt someone else."

A BOLO, short for "be on the lookout," alert was issued for the suspect, believed to be on the run, and the vehicle he drove. In the meantime, forensics was called in to do a more thorough search of Jamieson's house. Though more crystal meth and drug paraphernalia were discovered, along with some rope that could have been used as the ligature in the strangulations, there was no sign of Roger's stolen firearm that Dylan had hoped to recover in bolstering the case against the suspect. But he was obviously smart enough to get rid of the weapon. That notwithstanding, the evidence pointed squarely toward Jamieson as Roger's killer and Dylan knew that every second counted in the search for him.

NAOMI HAD A sense that something was up, even if she couldn't put a finger on it. Call it women's intuition. Or the strange yet satisfying look on Dylan's handsome face. She suspected it went beyond the lovemaking that kept them going for much of last night. Or the powerful vibes of deep affection that seemed to resonate between them in the process that could no longer be denied. So what then?

"We've got him…" Dylan clutched her shoulders and grinned as they stood in the great room. "The man who killed your uncle is now in custody."

Naomi's face lit with shock. "When? How? Who is he?"

"His name is Zachary Jamieson," explained Dylan. "He's a florist employee and one of our original suspects. Hidden inside his house, where he lived alone, we found the .45 ACP handgun used to shoot Roger." Dylan let that sink in as she contemplated the enormity of the news. "There's more irrefutable evidence tying Jamieson to the Violet Killer case. A latent palm print found on a tennis bracelet worn by Sylvie Maguire, the latest murder victim, when she was killed, belonged to Jamieson. He must have sensed that the walls were closing in on him. When we went to arrest him, he was already on the run."

"And how did you manage to capture him?" Naomi gazed at Dylan curiously, knowing how elusive the man had been for two years and counting.

"Once we were able to identify the unsub, Jamieson lost his uncanny ability to operate in plain view. We put out an all-points bulletin for his arrest. It didn't take long for the car Jamieson was driving to be spotted. After a short chase, he was forced to come to a stop in the parking lot of a convenience store. Once he stepped outside the vehicle, heavily armed police and FBI agents were waiting and swarmed him like bees on honey. Wisely, Jamieson surrendered without incident."

Naomi sucked in a deep breath. "So, it's over?" she dared ask.

"Actually, it's only just begun," Dylan corrected her, though she was sure he got her meaning. "We need to interrogate the suspect and see what he's willing to give us. Then he'll face justice and be punished accordingly for his crimes. Long process, but we're loaded and ready to go."

"Good." The knowledge that the perp who murdered her uncle was off the streets was slightly over-whelming to Naomi, but still a big relief. Not only for her, but the loved ones of the other victims of the serial killer.

"If you'd like to sit this one out, in terms of see-ing the suspect in person, I'll understand," Dylan voiced sympathetically.

"I wouldn't." She batted her lashes boldly. "I need to get a look at him to be able to put this behind me, to the extent that's possible."

"All right." He held her gaze intently and Naomi wondered what else was on his mind. Maybe he was considering where things stood between them as they moved forward. This weighed on her, as well. Only time would tell, but she believed they had turned a corner in their relationship and, for her part, there was no turning back.

Without prelude, Naomi lifted her mouth and kissed him. "Shall we go?"

DYLAN STOOD BETWEEN Naomi and Patricia, watch-ing through the one-way glass as the suspect sat in the interrogation room. Zachary Jamieson was me-dium sized and about six feet tall in leisurewear. The bushy-browed, blue-eyed florist worker had beige-blond hair in a taper faded on the sides, short quiff style. Dylan tried to picture him as the elusive serial homicidal psychopath they had been after for two years. Though at a glance, Jamieson may not have seemed like the prototype for their killer, Dylan real-ized that serial killers came in all shapes, shades and sizes. Anyone could fit the bill if motivated enough to become a killing machine. Detective Hwang sat across from the suspect, nibbling at the edges in seeing what he could derive from him, before Dylan and Patricia took their turn at bat grilling him. Jamieson had yet to be formally charged, which would likely necessitate lawyering up, limiting what he might say.

"Does he look familiar at all?" Dylan asked Naomi, noting Patricia's theory that they had probably crossed paths before.

Naomi studied the suspect carefully before turning away, as if too painful to look at further, and responded honestly. "Not really. Nothing's clicking. I mean, I suppose I could have passed him by here or there, but to say, yes, I know him—I can't..."

"It's fine." Dylan put his hand on hers, enjoying the touch of Naomi's soft skin. Just as he liked when their lips brushed before leaving his cabin. It told him that she was just as serious about seeing where things went with them as he was. This excited him as something to very much look forward to. But, right now, there was still unfinished business. "We have Jamieson dead to rights and can spare you needing to connect dots in any way."

"I agree," Patricia told her. "It looks like the perp has dug his own grave, so to speak, and he won't be able to climb out of it. Not this time."

To that end, Dylan felt relieved that without the benefit of Roger's deleted files, they were able to get Jamieson to uncharacteristically trip himself up with amateur missteps. Now they only needed to run with this and put the case to rest.

"I'm glad." Naomi faced him with a relaxed expression. "Now that the threat the serial killer posed to me and other women has been neutralized, I think I'll swing by my uncle's house for a bit."

"Really?" Dylan wondered if she had begun to tire of staying at his place. Was he reading her wrong in believing they were rebuilding something special?

"I need to go through his things," she explained, "and see what can be kept or donated or needs to be thrown away, before the house is put on the market."

So, she did plan to sell. He bristled at the thought. Did that mean her return to Miami was now imminent? Had he expected otherwise? Should he be surprised, even with the heated passions and more that they had enjoyed since she got back to town? Dylan realized that it didn't matter, as he was prepared to do whatever it took to be with her, if she wanted to be with him. "Sounds like a smart move on your part," he told her, feeling it should be safe enough for Naomi to go there on her own. "I'll come by and help as soon as I'm done here."

"That would be great." She smiled and glanced at Patricia, before gazing at Jamieson. "Good luck with him in there."

Patricia grinned. "Thanks. It's his luck that's run out."

Naomi nodded. "Hope so."

Dylan walked her out and returned, ready to go at the suspect in securing a confession on all fronts.

Chapter Seventeen

Dylan walked into the room, carrying two evidence bags. He placed them on the table and sat across from the handcuffed suspect in the same chair Hwang had occupied, before leaving the interrogation room on cue. It was left to Dylan to turn up the heat on Zachary Jamieson. He wasted no time in this regard. "I'm Detective Hester. You've been a busy man these past two years, Zach," he spoke curtly, following Hwang's lead. "Or would you prefer I call you Blue Violet?" He never gave the perp a chance to answer. "It's over now. Your best bet is to cooperate with us and maybe you can escape death row." In truth, Dylan knew that in Oregon, crimes qualifying for the death penalty in recent years generally did not include serial murders, such as those attributed to the suspect. If Jamieson didn't know that, it wouldn't hurt to use as leverage for now.

Jamieson snarled. "As I told the other detective, I have no idea what you're talking about. I didn't kill anyone, least of all Sylvie Maguire."

Dylan was undeterred. He slid a plastic evidence

bag containing a tennis bracelet toward the suspect. "This belonged to Sylvie Maguire. Your palm print was found on the murdered woman's bracelet. Can you explain that?"

"Yeah, I can," he said nonchalantly.

"This ought to be good." Dylan was barely able to suppress a sarcastic snicker.

Jamieson shifted in the chair, ill at ease. "I gave Sylvie that bracelet. It was a gift to a friend, nothing more."

Dylan rolled his eyes skeptically. "A gift?"

"Yeah. I knew she liked jewelry, so I bought it for her."

"Where did you buy it?" pressed Dylan.

"A jewelry store near the florist shop where I work. I paid for it with my credit card."

Dylan remained unconvinced but knew this could easily be checked out. Even if he and the victim were acquainted, the suspect could have had a beef with her and murdered her. Or strangled her, in spite of their supposed friendship, as a serial killer. "You say you were friends. Where did you meet Sylvie Maguire?"

"At the Owl Club. She tended bar there," Jamieson replied swiftly.

That much made sense to Dylan, believing that the Violet Killer likely had gotten to know at least some of his victims, luring them into a false sense of complacently, till ready to kill. He peered at the suspect. "Why did you run?"

"I panicked." Jamieson lowered his head. "When

I heard that Sylvie had been murdered the same day we were hanging out together, I figured I'd be blamed for her death." He took a deep, uneven breath. "Looks like I was right."

Dylan wasn't easily swayed by good actors—or even bad ones, for that matter. Serial killers were, by their very nature, cunning and good with denial. But he wasn't ready yet to throw the hammer at the suspect as the Violet Killer. Dylan grabbed the other evidence bag that held a .45 ACP handgun and put it in front of Jamieson. "Do you recognize this?"

He stared at the weapon, then glared at Dylan. "No. Why should I?"

"Because it was found in a box in your bedroom." Dylan waited a beat. "This gun was used to murder a private investigator named Roger Lincoln. Know anything about that?"

"I've never seen that gun before." Jamieson's face reddened. "No idea where it came from."

Dylan considered that the weapon had been cleaned of all prints, making it impossible to prove definitively that he was the shooter. That was hardly enough to let him off the hook. He glared at the man. "You've got to do better than that," Dylan said, repeating an at-times effective cliché.

"It's the truth," Jamieson maintained, setting his jaw. "Someone must be trying to set me up," he claimed in a panicked voice.

Dylan mulled over that possibility, small as it might be, as he glanced at the one-way mirror and wondered what his colleagues' take was on this. Was the suspect feeding him a bunch of lies? Or was there something to his story? "What size shoe do you wear?" he thought to ask, homing in on the stalking and text messages Naomi had endured.

"Eleven and a half." Jamieson cocked a brow. "Why?"

If this was true, it left Dylan contemplating if he could be working with someone else in perpetrating the murders. Though most serial killers worked alone, it wasn't unheard of that two or more persons had joined forces in committing homicidal acts of violence. The so-called Hillside Stranglers, Kenneth Bianchi and Angelo Buono Jr., and serial killer tandems Leonard Lake and Charles Ng, and Charlene and Gerald Gallego, came to mind. Could that be the case here? Or was Jamieson as their unsub climbing up the wrong tree?

NAOMI DROPPED BY Dylan's log cabin to grab her laptop, bottle of water and firearm. She didn't expect she would need the 9mm Glock on this occasion, but tucked it in her waistband holster to be on the safe side. She noted that the officer on duty on the grounds had been reassigned. That was quick, but not too surprising, she supposed, with a suspect in police custody and other assignments to take on. Naomi drove to the house she grew up in. Walking around inside, it almost felt like the first time since returning to Pebble Creek, having spent most of it tucked away at Dylan's place. She had mixed feelings being back there, remembering happier times, while also coming to terms with the fact that her uncle Roger was gone. Selling the house would be difficult, but also the right thing to do, given that she would not be living there and could not afford to maintain two places at once. Exactly where she would call home was still up in the air.

When her cell phone rang, Naomi took it out of the back pocket of her gabardine pants. She saw the caller was Sophia for a video chat and wondered if her Secret Service colleague had made any headway in retrieving the files from Uncle Roger's laptop. Since they had already identified the Violet Killer, Naomi doubted it mattered anymore what her uncle had uncovered.

"Hey," Naomi said, and immediately noticed the earnest look on Sophia's face. "What is it?"

"Sorry it took longer than I thought to get back to you," she said. "Fortunately, I was able to recover enough of the deleted files to give you what you wanted. I'm sending them to you now. Take a look on your laptop…"

"Okay." Heading up to her room with it, Naomi asked with interest, "Can you give me a hint?"

"I can do better than that." Sophia licked her lips. "Your uncle was able to find a major hole in the alibis of one of the suspects."

"Really?" Naomi set the laptop on the computer desk and positioned herself on the solid wood stool. "I assume you're referring to Zachary Jamieson, who was arrested today for Uncle Roger's murder and the deaths of nine women as the Violet Killer."

"I hadn't gotten the word." Sophia frowned. "Ac-

tually, the unsub your uncle fingered as the likely serial killer was a man named Blade Canfield."

Before Naomi could wrap her mind around this
revelation and pull up the files, she heard a noise
from inside the room. Looking up, she saw standing
there in denim jeans, a knit hoodie jacket and dark
sneakers a tall, lean man in his late twenties with a
short black side-swept messy hairstyle and sinister-
looking dark hooded eyes. In one gloved hand, he
was holding a gun pointed at her. The other hand held
a silk blue scarf—the kind Naomi imagined might
be used to strangle someone.

"Good to see you again, Naomi…" the man said
in an eerie tone of voice.

"CAN I HAVE a word?" Chief Frazier stuck his head
into the interrogation room with an unreadable expression.

Dylan nodded, and stood. He grabbed the bags
of evidence. "Be right back," he told the suspect.
Not that Zachary Jamieson was going anywhere for
the time being, as Dylan weighed whether or not he
was their unsub. Outside the room, in addition to the
chief, standing there were Agent Stabler, Detective
Hwang and George Suina. All looked tense, prompt-
ing Dylan to ask, "What's up?"

"There's been a new development," Frazier said
stiffly. "Actually, more than one." He scratched the
tip of his nose. "The Secret Service uncovered evidence in the Violet Killer case." He glanced at Patricia, deferring to her.

"Secret Service Agent Sophia Menendez, at Naomi's request, was able to recover relevant information in the death of Roger Lincoln and the serial homicides investigation," Patricia announced, a catch to her voice.

Dylan was happy to hear that Naomi's friend and coworker came through with something to help their case. "I'm listening…"

"It moves us away from Zachary Jamieson as our main suspect," she said, "and directly toward trust fund baby Blade Canfield. Roger was able to trip up Canfield's supposedly airtight alibis for his whereabouts during many of the murders. Using both legal and otherwise means, Roger gained access to bank accounts and money that went straight from Canfield to so-called witnesses who lied for him. This corresponded to some of the phone numbers we took from Roger's cell phone. At least one of the witnesses came clean to Roger and was prepared to testify against Canfield to that effect, before the man mysteriously vanished and can be presumed dead, if Canfield had his way of self-protection at all costs."

"Turns out Canfield recently sold a dark-colored SUV that matches the one Naomi reported was trying to run her off the road—or worse," Hwang stated. "The perp's been running rings around us for two years."

Dylan reacted to the shocking info. "No denying the strong circumstantial evidence here for Canfield's guilt as the Violet Killer," he said musingly. "It certainly appears to let Jamieson off the hook—for these crimes anyway." While seemingly pointing at Blade Canfield as the unsub. "But we need more concrete evidence to tie Canfield directly to the murders, if we're to put him away for good…" Dylan cautioned, not wanting the suspect to use his wealth to try to circumvent justice.

"We've got it," Suina chipped in. "Just received notification from CODIS that they found a match for the crime scene DNA taken from beneath the nails of murder victim Sandra Neville. It matched Blade Canfield's DNA that was collected after an arrest eight years ago, following a brawl at a bar that left the other person with a broken jaw. Charges were ultimately dropped, as the victim apparently refused to testify. It was believed that Canfield bought his way out of trouble."

"Not this time," Dylan snorted; the DNA match was just what they needed to beat the perp at his own deadly game. "It's time he's finally held accountable for his crimes." It suddenly occurred to Dylan that Naomi was still in danger. "Naomi's at Roger's house, which she now owns," he clarified. "If Blade Canfield sees this as an opening to go after her—"

"Then he will likely act on his dark impulses and anomalous fixation on Naomi," Patricia argued.

"We've already put out a warrant for Canfield's immediate arrest," Frazier declared. "My guess is that he's probably already figured out the walls are starting to close in. If he's smart—and Canfield seems to think he is—he'll be more interested in saving his own neck than anything else, by skipping town."

"That's an assumption I'm not willing to gamble

Naomi's life on," Dylan stated flatly, his heart skipping a beat at the mere thought of Canfield catching her off guard. He took out his cell phone and called her. *Answer*, he pleaded after several rings, before it went to voice mail. Dylan cursed within and left her a message, updating her on the investigation and Blade Canfield as a serious person of interest, warning her to be on the lookout for the extremely dangerous suspect. "I need a SWAT team to go to Naomi's address posthaste," Dylan ordered, thinking Canfield could try to take her as a hostage, if cornered. "I'm heading over there myself," he said, praying it wasn't too late to tell Naomi everything he felt for her and was willing to do to make them a couple for a lifetime.

"I'm going with you," Patricia told him. The sharp look in her determined eyes told him there was no room for argument.

"Let's go," Dylan said succinctly.

"What about him?" Hwang asked, pointing through the one-way window at Zachary Jamieson.

Dylan glanced at the suspect. "Let him sit there till we can check and recheck any and everything about him and any possible role he may have played in the Violet Killer case." They were not about to let a guilty man slip through their fingertips. Even if the number one suspect as the Violet Killer was now Blade Canfield, who could be targeting Naomi as his next violet to snuff out like a delicate flower.

Chapter Eighteen

Naomi's first instinct was to go for her weapon. She figured that she had a decent chance to get off one round, maybe two, that could stop the intruder in his tracks before he ever knew what hit him. But she also knew that even with him pointing a gun at her haphazardly while also dangling a scarf, he would likely still be able to fire it and hit her at least once. That one time could prove fatal. Then she would never get the opportunity to make things right with Dylan, in professing her love and strong desire to build a life together. It was with that fervent hope in mind that Naomi decided it best not to throw caution to the wind. Not yet. She figured if the perp had intended to kill her immediately, he would already have done so.

"I'll take that," he said tersely, snatching the cell phone from her grasp. It was just as Dylan was phoning, before it went to voice mail. "You won't be needing this anymore."

Naomi watched the intruder shut the phone off and hurl it at the wall as if to see how far it could bounce off. Would Dylan sense that something was wrong? Had Sophia reported the interruption of their phone call? Regardless, Naomi feared she was on her own at present in dealing with the dire situation she was in. "Do we know each other?" she asked the man inquisitively, in considering his own words to that effect, *"Good to see you again, Naomi..."* Naomi studied him as she continued to sit on the stool, as if stuck like adhesive, while he hovered like a portentous shadow. Sophia said his name was Blade Canfield. Naomi recalled that he was one of the Violet Killer suspects the Task Force had put together. Was he friends or even partners in crime with Zachary Jamieson?

"Guess you don't remember." The man frowned, as if disappointed. "Why am I not surprised? Two years ago, at a club, I tried to strike up a conversation, but you just blew me off."

She peered at him, trying to put the face into her memory. Not normally one to blow off someone who was respectful in initiating a chat, Naomi suspected that he was not. Then there was the fact that she was dating Dylan at the time and would not have been interested in giving any other man false encouragement. "I'm sorry," she told him, trying to sound as sincere as possible. As if this might somehow get him to back off. Or give her a better opportunity to go on the attack.

"Yeah, I'll bet." He rolled his eyes. "Actually, you did yourself a favor. You were supposed to be my first victim. Practice makes perfect and all that. But you left town before I could put my plan into action. Another unfortunate violet had to take your place. And another and another—till I really got into a groove. Imagine how shocked I was when I stole Roger Lincoln's laptop after killing him—and discovered that the very person he was talking to just before his death was you, the violet of my dreams." He laughed whimsically. "Seemed like the stars found a way to line up again much to my liking. All I needed to do was be patient. Looks like it paid off big-time, as you came back to this house with no security system in place and without backup, as if to sign your own death warrant—"

Naomi was stunned beyond belief. He had planned to murder her before she moved to Miami? How had she been so fortunate to escape his deadly desires? Had she stuck around, could she have been able to somehow stop him before he could kill other women? Her uncle Roger? And had she now come full circle so this lunatic ended up murdering her anyway, as if her fate had been sealed two years in the making?

"I know it's a lot to take in," he said wryly. "But it is what it is. Anyway, for the record, my name's Blade Canfield. But I guess you already know that, thanks to your friend." He cursed and contorted his features. "Should have done a better job making sure those files from your uncle's laptop could never be recovered. Now that the cat's out of the bag, it's forced me to have a change of plans. Oh well, what's done is done."

"That's true." Naomi's voice shook disconcertingly. She could only imagine what his previous or current plans were for her. Neither had to be good, considering the outcome for the other women he'd targeted. She hoped against hope that she might be able to reason with him somehow to buy needed time. "So, maybe you should just quit while you're ahead and go somewhere else in the world, where no one can ever find you. After all, you have the resources, right?" Having money to burn, by all accounts, gave him some leeway in planning an escape.

"You'd like that, wouldn't you?" Canfield chuckled derisively. "Sorry, no can do." He waved the gun precariously. "By the way, in case you didn't recognize it, this happens to be your uncle's Blackhawk .44 Magnum revolver. I thought it would be appropriate to use to finish you off." He raised the silk scarf. "Unless, I decide to strangle you with this instead, like I did the other hapless women who fell into my trap with no means to escape. Haven't decided yet. Fortunately, I'm in no hurry." He held up the weapon again that belonged to Naomi's uncle—another hard pill to swallow—making her weak in the knees and wondering if he would use it to kill her as well in a strange irony. "I needed to ditch my own firearm— planting it in the bedroom of a patsy named Zachary Jamieson I set up to take the fall for the death of Lincoln and my last violet victim, Sylvie Maguire. Ingenious, truly. Jamieson made it almost too easy to befriend, only to strangle the unsuspecting Sylvie after he left her place, knowing the cops would pin the blame on him. Which they did and, by extension, the other murders perpetrated by the infamous Violet Killer."

Canfield laughed, obviously pleased with himself. Then, just as quickly, his countenance darkened bitterly. "But, no thanks to you, it appears as though your boyfriend, Detective Hester, and his fellow police, FBI and Secret Service counterparts are on to me. Too little, too late, I'm afraid. At least for you…" He pointed the gun straight at her face. "Get up!" She hesitated to do so, fearing he might shoot her on the spot. "Now!" His voice echoed throughout the room.

Naomi got to her feet slowly while weighing her options. Did she go for broke now and reach for her weapon? Or at a later opportunity, assuming there was one? Had Dylan figured it all out and was planning a countermove to thwart the serial killer's plans before he was able to kick them into gear? "Oh, and I assume you're packing," Canfield said, as though reading her mind. "I would be, if I were you. Turn around," he ordered. "And don't try anything stupid, if you value your life."

Naomi very much valued her life and any future she might have with Dylan. As such, she did as Canfield demanded, believing that he was too full of himself and obsessed with her to simply shoot her in the back of the head and call it a day. Still, she closed her eyes, the life Naomi still wanted flashing before her like a motion picture in vivid color, as he came up behind her, placing the cold barrel of the gun to her cheek. He removed the firearm from her holster, tucking it away in his jacket pocket. "Good girl," he said succinctly. "Now move..."

Naomi felt the gun poke her in the back as she headed out of the room and down the hall and stairs, with Canfield right there every step of the way. "Where are you taking me?" she hesitated to ask, as they reached the first floor. Would he try to use her as a bargaining chip to get out of town? Or did the killer have something more sinister in mind?

"Not very far," Canfield said, shoving her out the door. "We're just going to take a little walk out into the woods."

"And then what?" Naomi challenged him, reading between the thin lines.

"Then I'll let you live, once I no longer need you as an insurance policy, and I'll escape to my car waiting for me at the top of the hill—and you'll never see me again..."

She wasn't buying it. He planned to kill her, to feed his ego and add to his murderous conquests. Then flee, to leave Dylan to find her body and be broken for what might have been and frustrated that he had once again been outfoxed by the Violet Killer. She couldn't allow that to happen. "You won't get away with this," she spat, if only to throw him off his game a bit.

"When have I heard that before?" he mocked her, pushing her forward again. "I think I will, as always, and there's no one to stop me. At least, not this day."

Naomi hated his confidence, stemming from being able to successfully terrorize the town for two

years. This would backfire on him, she was sure. But
would it be too late for her to escape his lunacy? "It
was you watching me in the lake, wasn't it?" she
asked to be sure, as they headed toward the trees.

"Yeah, I confess," Canfield conceded. "Couldn't
resist checking you out, while keeping you on edge
at the same time. Same was true with the text messages and when I stayed on your tail one day with
my SUV after you drove from Hester's cabin, before
allowing you to escape unharmed. Half the fun has
been playing with your head. Guess the two-year
delay has been well worth the wait."

Naomi cringed as he validated her beliefs and
further connected the dots in tying him to the murders. She looked over her shoulder and asked, in an
effort to keep him talking, "So, what's with the violets anyway? Are they just something you dreamed
up to leave in the victims' mouths for the shock factor? Or is there another deep-seated reason for that?"

"I admire your curiosity, Secret Service Agent
Lincoln." Canfield chuckled. "Doesn't hurt to in-
dulge you. No, there is no abused-as-a child or
rejected-as-an-adult or some psychological mumbo-
jumbo explanation. The truth of the matter is that I
happen to appreciate the delicacies of violets, which
is akin to the ladies I chose to put out to pasture. The
violet as a going-away present seemed most apropos, while at the same time giving the cops fits in
trying to figure it out." He chortled wickedly. "I see
it's catching."

"Don't flatter yourself," Naomi shot back, hoping

to catch him off guard. "I'm not a big fan of violets, no matter the use. What you choose to do with them is your business."

"Glad to see we're on the same page," he quipped, shoving her ahead roughly.

When they were deep enough into the woods, Naomi was certain that he would strangle her, in keeping in line with the other victims' fate, shooting her only as a last resort. She needed to make her move to prevent either occurrence. Or die trying.

As HE SPED through traffic, Dylan wanted to kick himself for jumping the gun in assuming they had the unsub in Zachary Jamieson. Even if the pieces fit at the time, they may have fit too perfectly. All the more reason Dylan felt he should have, at the very least, questioned the assumptions. Had he left the door open, he would not have essentially given Naomi a coast-is-clear message, putting her own life in jeopardy.

"How did we not see Blade Canfield for who he truly was?" Dylan faced Patricia in the passenger seat.

"Because he worked overtime to keep that from happening," the profiler responded, having just tried to call Naomi, to no avail. "That's classic among smart serial killers. Canfield weaved an elaborate labyrinth that kept us going around in circles. Fortunately, Roger Lincoln was able to figure things out. Some of his methods may have been questionable, but no one can argue with the results, thanks to the Secret Service computer whiz finding a way to crack his computer files."

"I agree," Dylan said, giving a mental thumbs-up to Sophia Menendez. She definitely did right by Naomi in giving them what she promised, and then some, including an alert that she had been cut off in a phone chat with Naomi and feared she was in danger. He pressed down on the accelerator to move faster, knowing that every second was one second less needed to reach his destination before it was too late. "Can you try calling Naomi again?" he asked Patricia, hoping that she still had access to her phone and could help them help her.

"Will do," she said. Again, no response, frustrating them both.

As he approached a blue BMW X6 parked off the side of the road on the hill, Dylan's first thought was that it might have been abandoned. But, given the high cost of the luxury vehicle, that seemed unlikely. It then occurred to him that the car was simply left there as a temporary measure, till the driver returned and could then leave in a hurry without much attention. Blade Canfield came to mind. On an uneasy hunch, Dylan pulled up behind the car. He called into the Pebble Creek PD and requested they run the plate number.

"The vehicle is registered to a Blade Nicholas Canfield," the dispatcher said momentarily.

Dylan's heart skipped a beat as they got out of the car, with their weapons drawn. Both wore bullet-resistant vests as they moved toward the vehicle. No one was inside. "Canfield's gone after Naomi at her house," he said knowingly.

"And this is to be his escape route," the FBI profiler uttered.

"If anything happens to Naomi…" Dylan found himself unable to finish the thought, as losing her just when he had found her again, only this time with no more tomorrow, was more than he could bear.

"Don't give up hope," insisted Patricia. "We can still get to her before Canfield can carry out his homicidal urges against the object of his fixation."

Dylan had to believe that, as he was determined to stay optimistic that everything would work out and Naomi would be unharmed when this was over. "I won't," he promised. "We'll proceed on foot, so as not to alert Canfield, and head to the house through the woods."

"I was thinking the same thing," she told him.

They started down the hill, when Dylan spotted some movement in the trees. It was Naomi and Canfield. He was forcing her to walk at gunpoint. Patricia saw it, too. She took out her firearm. "It's better that we split up and hit him from two angles, if need be."

"I agree," Dylan said, lifting the pistol from his holster. He motioned for her to move in one direction, while he went in another. All one of them needed was a clear shot and they could take down the serial killer before he could lay a finger on Naomi.

Moving stealthily down the knoll, Dylan was determined to make sure the love of his life lived to see another day. Make that many more days, weeks,

months and years. They had come too far in rebuilding a relationship to see it end prematurely. He made
his way into the woods, careful not to tip his hand,
sure the same was true for Patricia. The preferred
thing would be to keep Canfield alive to answer for
his crimes. But if it came to saving him or Naomi,
Dylan never flinched in knowing which was the only
real choice.

He watched from behind a tall cottonwood tree,
gun aimed and prepared to shoot, as Canfield and
Naomi stopped walking. She turned to face the serial
killer, who put his own firearm in his jacket pocket,
replacing it with a scarf. "Sorry, I lied," Canfield
told Naomi coldly, as he flexed the scarf between
his hands. "I can't let you live. It'll be too much fun
watching you die and then getting away once again."

Naomi sneered defiantly and retorted, "I lied, too,
when I told you I wouldn't put up a fight. Bring it
on."

Just as Dylan was ready to intervene, spotting Patricia coming up fast, both watched with amazement
as Naomi used a mixture of old-fashioned hand-to-
hand combat and jujitsu to take down her opponent.
When Canfield tried to go for his gun, she kicked it
away effortlessly. He reached inside his jacket pocket
for a second gun, which Dylan suspected was Naomi's own confiscated firearm. She easily dislodged
it from his hand and used her attacker's desperate
and futile attempts to regain the upper hand against
him, till he was fully subdued.

Taking no chances, Dylan announced his and

Agent Stabler's presence and rushed toward them. Seeing him, Naomi's eyes lit and she fell into his arms. "What took you so long?" she cried lightheartedly.

He laughed a little as Patricia made sure her abductor and a killer stayed down, if not out. "Got here as soon as I could," Dylan told Naomi. "But looking at the way you manhandled the perp, it seems like you had things well in hand."

"Desperate times called for desperate measures," she quipped, still clinging to him as if being apart was unbearable. He felt the same way. "There's Uncle Roger's firearm," Naomi indicated, nodding her head at the weapon the assailant had been carrying, resting comfortable in the dirt. "It was apparently going to be his ace in the hole if he was unable to strangle me to death."

Dylan eyed the second firearm on the ground. "I take it the other gun belongs to you?"

"Yes, he took it from me under threat of death," she moaned. "Can't wait to reclaim, once it's been processed as part of a crime scene."

"Shouldn't take long." Dylan furrowed his brow at the mere thought of Canfield succeeding in his deadly endeavor. Using Roger's .44 Magnum revolver as a weapon against Naomi would have made it even worse, after having murdered her uncle before Naomi's very eyes. "Thank goodness Canfield fell short on both counts."

"Tell me about it," she stated without humor.

Patricia handcuffed the serial killer. "We've

got him!" the FBI agent declared victoriously. She chuckled while helping a dazed and bruised Canfield to his feet. "Or should I say, you did, Secret Service Special Agent Lincoln."

"Only did what I had to," Naomi said modestly. "Thanks for having my back."

"It's my job and honor." Patricia showed her teeth. "We all had each other's backs in bringing down this vile creature."

"Couldn't agree more," Dylan seconded, before reading Canfield his rights as the SWAT unit and other law enforcement converged on the scene and took the scowling prisoner away.

"Did he hurt you at all?" Dylan asked once they were back at the house alone.

"No, not really," Naomi responded, ignoring the soreness in her back from some poking and prodding by the serial killer. "But not from lack of trying."

"I'm sorry it had to come to that."

"It could've been much worse." She frowned thoughtfully. "Canfield gleefully admitted that he had actually targeted me for his first kill two years ago."

Dylan's expression hardened with shock. "You can't be serious?"

"He claimed we met at a club, but I balked at his advances—which apparently were little more than a ruse to get me alone to practice the sick art of murder. I left for Miami before Canfield could take another crack at me."

Dylan cursed beneath a deep breath. "The mere thought that he could've killed you back then, depriving you of a future you deserved…"

"He didn't, though," Naomi pointed out gratefully.

"We dropped the ball in prematurely putting it all on Zachary Jamieson," Dylan muttered with annoyance.

"Don't beat yourself up over it," she stressed sympathetically, against his inclination to blame himself for not catching the killer sooner. "Canfield had us all fooled. He confessed to setting Jamieson up with the weapon used to kill Uncle Roger, along with killing Sylvie Maguire and the other women. Canfield also admitted to being the one who sent the text messages, was stalking me by the lake and was the driver of the dark SUV."

"Just as we'd ascertained through the clues he left behind." Dylan shook his head, clearly still annoyed with the revelations nevertheless. "The perp knew no boundaries in his criminal behavior and wicked mind."

"True enough," concurred Naomi, having lived through it and coming out on top. "But he overplayed his hand and finally ran out of luck."

Dylan nodded. "We owe you for that, Naomi. I don't think the perp ever saw what was coming when he attempted to strangle you."

She chuckled. "Given that I feared for my life, he gave me no other option but to put my training to good use." That notwithstanding, Naomi felt comforted in knowing that Dylan and Patricia were prepared to take Canfield out, had she been unable to bring him down herself.

"We'll need you to come downtown to make an official statement," Dylan said gingerly. "If you want to wait till tomorrow—"

"I don't," she told him emphatically. "No time like the present. The sooner you have whatever you need to make sure Blade Canfield rots away behind bars, the better."

"Thought you might say that." Dylan pulled her into his arms, giving her a quick peck on the mouth. "Between the serial murders, kidnapping and attempted murder, and maybe stalking thrown in for good measure, I'm pretty sure that Canfield's days of wreaking havoc on our community are over!"

Naomi found comfort in those words as she kissed him this time, even as her thoughts turned to other matters of the heart that still needed to be fully addressed and responded to by Dylan, accordingly.

BY THAT EVENING, when things had settled down and they were alone at Dylan's log cabin, safe and sound, Naomi felt it incumbent upon herself to put all her cards on the table, knowing just how easily this moment in time could have slipped away forever without Dylan realizing exactly where she stood in her strong feelings for him. She wasn't about to allow anything—or anyone—else to come between them.

"I have something I need to tell you, Dylan..." she began eagerly as they stood in the living room.

"Me first." He held up a hand while regarding her in earnest.

"Uh, okay." She met his gaze intently.

"Here goes…" Dylan gave a deep sigh. "Two years ago, I foolishly let you get away without conveying what I should have. Now I'd like a redo, and hope it's not too late." He took a box out of his pocket, opened it and, to Naomi's surprise, removed a pear-shaped diamond ring. "I've been saving this for the past two years, hoping I might someday be able to give it to you. That day has come." He calmly placed the ring on her trembling finger. "I'm asking you to marry me, Naomi. But before you respond, I wanted you to know that I'm prepared to move to Miami, in support of your career with the Secret Service. I love my job, but not nearly as much as I love you. I can catch on with the Miami PD. Or find some other line of work, I don't care. I only want to spend the rest of my life with you as my wife and mother to any children we wish to bring into this world." Dylan gave an anxious grin. "You can tell me what you're thinking now."

Naomi could barely hold back tears in digesting his heartfelt words and what he was willing to sacrifice to make her his wife. It told her all she needed to know about the man, making her own decision only that much more satisfying. She stared mesmerizingly at the engagement ring, set in 14K rose gold. It was a perfect fit and was right where the ring belonged. Gazing up into Dylan's eyes, Naomi uttered, "What I'm thinking is that while I love working for the Secret Service, it falls short of what I really need in my life to be happy—and that's you."

He cocked a brow nervously. "So, what are you saying?"

She flashed her teeth. "I'm saying that I love you, Dylan Hester, and yes, yes, yes, I'll marry you a thousand times, wherever we chose to call home!"

"Seriously?" He broke into a big grin.

"As serious as I've ever been in my life," she promised him.

"You've made me the happiest man." Dylan gave her a mouthwatering kiss, which Naomi returned in full, before he pulled back. He eyed her curiously. "But how do you want this to go with the job situation?"

Holding his gaze, she responded, having given it some long consideration. "I plan to retire from the Secret Service and reopen Uncle Roger's private investigation agency. I can put my skills to good use, with some worthwhile investigations and consultancy work." She put her ring hand in his. "I was hoping we could go into business together. I'm sure my uncle would've approved had he been given the opportunity to show his support. But if you prefer to keep working with the Pebble Creek Police Department, that's fine by me. Having you as my husband is more than I could ask for at this stage of my life. Anything else would be a bonus."

"Then it's a bonus you shall have." Dylan took her into his arms. "It would be my pleasure to partner up with you in keeping Roger's private investigation firm alive. Working with the Pebble Creek PD had its rewards, but they can't compare with taking on this exciting new venture, side by side with my wife. So, yes, count me in, Naomi."

He kissed her again with even more yearning that packed a spine-tingling punch, and she reciprocated in kind, before telling him again just how much she cherished his love and gave as much or more back to him. And would do so for the rest of her life.

Epilogue

The sixty-foot power cruiser sat still on the lake on a sunny Saturday afternoon on a day in late June. It was a dream come true for Dylan Hester, courtesy of his mentor, Roger Lincoln, who left funds in his will to help make it happen. Sharing the boat and all its comforts and joys was Dylan's wife, Naomi, who was two months' pregnant with their first child. The co-owners of Lincoln and Hester Investigations were taking a break from their day-to-day married and professional lives to spend some time on the water with family and friends. It was a welcome respite after dealing with the long trial and conviction of serial killer Blade Canfield, who due in part to the testimony of Naomi, the state's star witness, would be spending the rest of his life behind bars at Oregon State Penitentiary. His high-powered defense proved to be no match for the strong case presented by the prosecution for his guilt. Once his fate had been sealed, Canfield began to sing like a canary, practically bragging about his road to homicidal tendencies. This prompted FBI profiler Patricia Stabler to write a true-crime book on the perp, swept up in the desire to add to the annals of serial killer psychopaths. Cleared in the Violet Killer investigation was onetime suspect Zachary Jamieson, but he was still contending with drug possession charges.

Dylan stood on the deck, taking in the magnificent view while counting his blessings. First and foremost was having the love of his life, Naomi, as his wife, lover and best friend, to experience the highs and lows of life, wherever they took them. They had survived a two-year separation and a crazed killer to find their way back to one another, and were the better for it. He couldn't imagine a life without her and, thankfully, wouldn't have to.

"I'm glad you didn't let Naomi get away this time, little brother," Dylan's sister, Stefany, whispered in his ear from behind, as though reading his mind. She and her husband, Theodore, had flown in from Africa to spend a little time with Dylan and his bride, for some relaxation and fishing.

Grinning, he turned Stefany's way and replied, "Hey, I learned from the best. With you and yours as a guide to a happy marriage, it was only a matter of time before I got smart enough to follow suit."

Stefany laughed. "Better late than never."

It was a philosophy Dylan agreed with wholeheartedly, as Naomi and the little bundle she was carrying meant everything to him and so much more.

"YOU LOOK POSITIVELY GLOWING!" Sophia Menendez uttered to Naomi, as they sat on the sectional sofa in the air-conditioned console below deck.

"Oh, really?" Naomi batted her eyes, flattered. She was thrilled that her former roommate and fellow agent with the Secret Service had decided to pay her a visit, accompanied by Sophia's drop-dead gorgeous, tall, dark and handsome boyfriend, Lucas Etheridge. Moreover, Naomi enjoyed the feeling of being a wife to a terrific, hardworking guy in Dylan, as well as impending motherhood, now that their first child was on the way. They had spoken about having a couple of more children down the line but, for now, being in the company of each other was more than she could have asked for in a partner. "I'll take that as a compliment," she teased Sophia.

"It definitely is," her friend made clear. "Between that brilliant complexion, your cute new ginger-curls hairstyle, glow of pregnancy and power of love, what's not to compliment."

"Can't argue with you there." Naomi laughed, resisting the urge to feel her belly, something that Dylan had perfected of late. She had no doubt he would make a great dad, just as he made a marvelous husband. In the post Blade Canfield/Violet Killer era, both had been able to successfully transition from their respective jobs with the Secret Service and the Pebble Creek Police Department to carry on with her uncle Roger's detective agency. They brought it to a new level by expanding the types of investigations and using social media to build their brand. As a result, they were able to work on starting a family and building bridges with others they were close to, while making Dylan's lakefront log cabin their home as a couple with Naomi adding her own touches to truly belong.

"Doesn't mean we don't miss you like crazy at the Secret Service," Sophia said, making a somber face to express such. "Even Jared has recognized what an asset you were to the agency. If you ever want to get back in, we'd love to have you."

Naomi beamed, a good feeling to know she was appreciated by her former employer. Especially her old boss and Sophia herself. "Thanks, but no thanks," she told her in a heartfelt tone of voice. "As much as I enjoyed performing my duties for the agency and miss working with you, in particular, I'm so much happier in my new life as Mrs. Dylan Hester and soon to be a doting mom."

"Figured as much." Sophia chuckled. "Just thought I'd put it out there."

"And I love you for it, girlfriend." Naomi gave her a toothy smile. "As for the Secret Service, I'll settle for being able to tap into your expertise from time to time when working a case." She was mindful of Sophia's amazing efforts, along with Naomi's uncle Roger, in helping to make the case against Blade Canfield.

"Anytime!" Sophia promised, grinning back.

"Well, let's not keep our men waiting any longer," Naomi said, eager to wrap herself in Dylan's welcoming arms.

Sophia agreed. "Yes, let's not."

They both stood and went back up to the main deck, where Naomi wasted no time going to the man of her dreams come true. Dylan did not disappoint, laying a solid kiss on her that left little doubt that she belonged to him and only him for the rest of their lives.

* * * * *

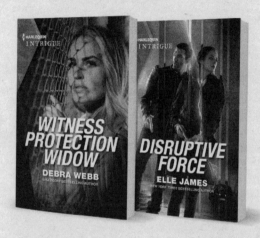

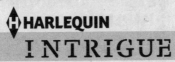

*When a young woman is discovered buried alive,
Colorado ME Dr. Chloe Pascale knows that the
relentless serial killer she barely escaped has found her.
To stop him, she must trust police chief
Weston Ford with her darkest secrets. But getting
too close is putting their guarded hearts at risk—and
leading into an inescapable trap...*

*Read on for a sneak preview of
Grave Danger,
part of the Defenders of Battle Mountain series
from Nichole Severn.*

Three months ago...
When I'm done, you're going to beg me for the pain.

Chloe Pascale struggled to open her eyes. She blinked against
the brightness of the sky. Trees. Snow. Cold. Her head pounded in
rhythm to her racing heartbeat. Shuffling reached her ears as her
last memories lightninged across her mind like a half-remembered
dream. She'd gone out for a run on the trail near her house. Then...
Fear clawed at her insides, her hands curling into fists. He'd come
out of the woods. He'd... She licked her lips, her mouth dry. He'd
drugged her, but with what and how many milliliters, she wasn't
sure. The haze of unconsciousness slipped from her mind, and a
new terrifying reality forced her from ignorance. "Where am I?"

Dead leaves crunched off to her left. Her attacker's dark outline
shifted in her peripheral vision. Black ski mask. Lean build. Tall.
Well over six feet. Unfamiliar voice. Black jeans. His knees popped
as he crouched beside her, the long shovel in his left hand digging

into the soil near her head. The tip of the tool was coated in mud. Reaching a gloved hand toward her, he stroked the left side of her jawline, ear to chin, and a shiver chased down her spine against her wishes. "Don't worry, Dr. Miles. It'll be all over soon."

His voice… It sounded…off. Disguised?

"How do you know my name? What do you want?" She blinked to clear her head. The injection site at the base of her neck itched, then burned, and she brought her hands up to assess the damage. Ropes encircled her wrists, and she lifted her head from the ground. Her ankles had been bound, too. She pulled against the strands, but she couldn't break through. Then, almost as though demanding her attention, she caught sight of the refrigerator. Old. Light blue. Something out of the '50s with curves and heavy steel doors.

"I know everything about you, Chloe. Can I call you Chloe?" he asked. "I know where you live. I know where you work. I know your running route and how many hours you spend at the clinic. You really should change up your routine. Who knows who could be out there watching you? As for what I want, well, I'm going to let you figure that part out once you're inside."

Pressure built in her chest. She dug her heels into the ground, but the soil only gave way. No. No, no, no, no. This wasn't happening. Not to her. Darkness closed in around the edges of her vision, her breath coming in short bursts. Pulling at the ropes again, she locked her jaw against the scream working up her throat. She wasn't going in that refrigerator like the other victim she'd heard about on the news. Dr. Roberta Ellis. Buried alive, killed by asphyxiation. Tears burned in her eyes as he straightened and turned his back to her to finish the work he'd started with the shovel.

Don't miss
Grave Danger by Nichole Severn,
available February 2022 wherever
Harlequin books and ebooks are sold.

Harlequin.com

Get 4 FREE REWARDS!

We'll send you 2 FREE Books plus 2 FREE Mystery Gifts.

Harlequin Intrigue books are action-packed stories that will keep you on the edge of your seat. Solve the crime and deliver justice at all costs.

FREE Value Over $20
